Silent
Protection

Sign of Love Series
Book 3

Tonya Clark

CHAPTER ONE

Darryn

"So, are you ever going to say yes when I ask you out?"

The voice comes from behind me. It flows over me like hot liquid, warming my entire body. My knees almost buckle. Bryce Brooksman has been asking me out for the past month.

We met the night of the bombing. His sister, Charliee, was a victim that night, when a popular Italian restaurant was blown up. My partner, Tom, and I were the paramedics that took care of Charliee when they uncovered her. Bryce pissed me off when he basically pushed me away trying to get to Charliee, but my anger had quickly vanished when I witnessed the tenderness he used toward his sister. Charliee is deaf and she has a hearing dog that was also involved in the explosion. She was going crazy wondering about where he

1

was and watching Bryce calm her down was amazing. He was so gentle and caring. On the ride to the hospital, he kept her calm, signing to her the whole time. No words were spoken between them, it was beautiful to watch. As we approached the hospital, Charliee had gone unconscious again. I will never forget the look in Bryce's eyes when he looked back at me, the fear that was behind those deep green eyes.

Before that night, I don't remember ever seeing Bryce on a call or at the hospital, but since then I swear we run into each other at least twice a week. Tonight, again, here I am finishing up from dropping off a patient and there he is.

"You haven't asked me out this time." I smile to myself, keeping my attention on the paper I'm filling out. I know if I turn around, I'm going to get lost in those eyes. It's been extremely hard saying no to this man because of those eyes.

My body goes from warm to hot when he takes a step closer to me and I can now feel him against my back. He is working today, I can feel his bulletproof vest against my back. My heart skips knowing why they wear those vests. The meaning behind them, the danger they imply that this man puts himself into every time he goes to work.

"If I ask, will you say yes?" He speaks into my ear, causing my body to shiver.

How can I feel this hot and shiver at the same time? The way my body reacts to this man scares the hell out of me. No man has ever had this kind of effect on me.

Reaching around me, Bryce takes the pen out of my hand and turns me around to face him. "Darryn, would you like to grab a drink with me one evening?"

Damn it, there are those eyes. Maybe I should just tell him the truth and then he will finally stop asking me out every time we run into each other. It's a sure method, works every time. Placing my hand onto his chest, I push him back a couple steps. We are both in uniform and we don't need to be that close, plus I can't think straight with him standing that close to me.

"Bryce, here is the problem. I know I'm always saying no, but it's not because I'm not interested." I watch as the corner of his mouth slants up in a smile. "Hold on, this isn't me saying yes, I'm sorry. I'm just going to tell you the reason I keep saying no, that way you don't keep wasting your time asking and I don't have to keep telling you no. I'm not unattached."

I watch his eyebrows shoot up. "Darryn, all you had to do was tell me you had a boyfriend and I wouldn't have kept asking. I'm not like that."

He starts to walk away from me. I should just let him go, let him think whatever he wants to think. What do I care if he thinks I already have a boyfriend? But, I can't. I don't want him thinking I've led him on or something.

"Bryce, wait, you don't understand."

He just keeps walking in the other direction. "I don't have a boyfriend, Bryce, I have a daughter!" I yell after him, drawing attention from everyone in hearing distance.

It does stop him, though. Turning around, he stares me down for a moment. Why does he look mad? "You have a daughter?"

Nodding, I want to crawl behind the counter and hide from all the attention we have now. "Look, I should have said something earlier."

I watch as he walks back toward me. "I have said no because I can't just go out for a night 'out on the town.' I have no one to watch her."

"Is that the only reason you have said no when I've asked you all of those times?"

"Yes!"

"Bryce, we have to go," Bryce's identical look-alike says as he comes through the emergency room doors in a hurry.

Bryce has a twin brother, Derrick. The two look exactly like each other. The first time I thought I saw Bryce here at the hospital, I made a little bit of a fool out of myself when I accused him of ignoring me. Saying he was still mad at me for the night we met and I yelled at him when we were working on his sister. I basically told him to get over himself.

Lucky for me, Derrick has a sense of humor. He figured it out pretty fast that I was thinking he was his brother. I think he liked it even more that he got to tell me I had the wrong brother. I wanted to slap them both when Bryce walked up a short time later and Derrick had to clue him in to what was going on, and they both just stood there laughing at me. Bryce asked me out the first time that night. I had no trouble then telling him no, I just wanted to slap the smiles off both their faces. From that night forward, I didn't make the mistake again. I can tell the two of them apart no matter if they are together or not. It's all in their eyes. Bryce has kind eyes, they are soft. Derrick has mischief in his eyes, they are more playful or flirty. They may be identical in looks, but their personalities are complete opposites.

"Can I have your phone, please?" Bryce holds out his hand to me.

I don't even ask why, I pull it out of my pocket and hand it to him.

I watch as he types on it and then hands it back to me. "You now have my number. Call me when you have a day off." He turns and walks away, following his brother outside.

"What was that all about?" Tom, my partner, asks, now standing next to me.

"Nothing." I quickly shove my phone back in my pocket.

"Well, if you are done flirting with the police officer, I have everything restocked and we are ready to roll."

"I wasn't flirting with him." I keep my eyes down, hoping he doesn't see the redness in my cheeks.

Tom is a great partner. He and his wife are the only people I can call friends since I moved here to Washington a year ago. They are both always trying to set me up on dates though. His wife has even offered to watch Kendall for me so that I could go out. If only it was all that simple. So many times I have almost opened up to them and told them everything, but the fear is still there. I have to keep my daughter safe!

CHAPTER TWO

Bryce

"So, did you ask her out again only to have her turn you down?" Derrick smiles over the hood of the car and then disappears as he takes the driver's seat.

"This time she didn't really turn me down," I inform him as I slide into the passenger seat.

"So she said yes?" He quickly starts the engine and pulls out of the parking lot, sirens now blaring.

"Where are we off to?"

"Car accident, don't change the subject." Derrick gives me that knowing look he has, the one that tells me he thinks I'm dealing him a bunch of crap.

"This is the third one this morning." I have no hope of seeing Darryn on this call, or they would have been called out the same time as us.

"Focus, brother. Did the paramedic finally put you out of your misery and say yes to going out with you?" Derrick keeps probing.

He isn't going to shut up until I tell him. I just know what he is going to say when I tell him she has a kid. "She told me she has a daughter. That's why she keeps telling me no, not because she isn't interested."

"A daughter?" Derrick gives me that look. The one that tells me he thinks I'm crazy.

"Yep!" I confirm, nodding my head.

We may be identical in looks, but we are nothing alike when it comes to women or relationships. Derrick is still good with playing the field. Nothing serious, in no way ready to be "tied down" as he would say. Where I'm the one who wants the relationship. One person to get to know, and maybe have a future with. Commitment doesn't scare me in the least. I've never dated anyone before with kids, but it doesn't scare me away.

There is something about Darryn that pulls at me. I've watched her as she works a scene, helping the injured. She is strong, in control. Even her partner kind of backs up and lets her run the show I've noticed. But when you are talking to her, there is something there behind her eyes. She's not as tough as she seems on the outside. Like she is carrying the world on her shoulders and she is ready to fall.

"So did she say no again?" Derrick breaks through my thoughts.

"I gave her my number and told her to call me when she has a day off."

"Are you sure you want to get involved with someone with a kid? That takes relationships to a whole new level, man."

"It's a date, Derrick, let's just start there first."

Pulling up to the accident, I'm saved from any further questions about Darryn. This one is bad. Multiple cars, fire-fighters are already on scene. Derrick and I instantly go to work, controlling traffic around the scene.

"Check out this text that I just got from Charliee." Derrick throws me his phone.

"Is she all right?" I ask before looking down. Panic shoots through my chest for a moment. Since that night of the restau-rant bombing and almost losing her, I will admit we have all been a little more protective over Charliee. Seeing her laying on the ground, blood everywhere, clothes burnt, it's an image I don't think I will ever get out of my head.

I know since then we have all smothered her a little. She has been out of the hospital for a couple weeks now, but she is home alone. We tried to get her to go to Mom and Dad's for a while but no, our stubborn, very independent sister wants to be home. Between Derrick and myself, our parents and her best friend, Jayden, she isn't alone for long. Charliee is trying to be a good sport about it, but I can tell she is over us all hovering around her all the time.

I read the text and then glare over at my brother. "I'm sure this has nothing to do with thanking the guys from that night and a lot to do with that firefighter, Travis. He went a couple times to visit her at the hospital."

"Look who is on call with us." Derrick points over to one of the fire engines that is on the scene. Everyone is mopping up right now.

Looking over, I spot Travis. He and one of the other fire-fighters were the ones who found Charliee that night, buried under some of the fallen building.

I throw Derrick back his phone. "She asked you."

"Thanks, man. That way I look like the bad guy for not helping her out."

I smile. "He isn't a bad guy," I defend Travis. If Charliee is going to be interested in someone, he seemed like a decent guy. I wouldn't tell her that, of course. No one is going to be good enough for our sister.

"So you're saying give her the information?"

"Give her a little bit of a hard time first. Then a warning and then give her the information. Don't just hand it over. Definitely don't make it easy on her." Charliee thinks she has us wrapped around her little finger. Maybe she does.

Charliee was born deaf. Derrick and I were only three when she was born. Learning sign language was part of learning how to talk for us. She learned how to talk just as fast as she learned to sign as well. Mom and Dad wanted to make sure nothing held her back and put her in speech therapy at the age of two. Whatever you do, don't talk around her and think just because she can't hear, she doesn't know what you are saying. As long as she can see your lips, she can read them. She has never wanted people treating her differently just because she can't hear. Half of the people who meet her have no idea she is deaf. Levi, her hearing dog, came into the family when she was a senior in high school. They haven't been apart since.

"Hey, you ready to head out of here? I'm starving." Derrick slaps me on the back, heading toward the car.

It's been nonstop all morning. Looking at my watch, it's hard to believe it's already after 2:00 in the afternoon. Pulling my phone out, I check to see if I have any missed calls or texts. Nothing, did I really think she was going to try and get ahold of me? Maybe I should have gotten her number. I saw the look in Darryn's eyes when she told me about having a kid. She figured that was a sure way to scare me away from asking her out any more. The reason I put my number in her phone instead of hers in mine was to show her it didn't make me change my mind about wanting to go out with her.

"Are you coming?" Derrick yelled at me from the car.

Shoving my phone back into my pocket, I walk over and get into the passenger side of the car. "Where do you want to eat?"

CHAPTER THREE

Darryn

"So did Bryce asked you out again?" Tom asks as we sit and eat lunch.

I shrug my shoulders.

"Come on, Darryn, how many times are you going to turn that man down? Do you want me to talk to him? Tell him to back off?" Tom offered.

This is one of the reasons why I love Tom, he is like a big brother. "No, I don't need you talking to him. Today I told him I have a kid, thinking that might scare him away. It usually works."

"Usually? I'm guessing not this time," Tom said, laughing.

I shake my head. "No, instead he put his number into my phone and told me to call him on my next day off."

"Well, I have to give it to the man, he is persistent. So, are you going to call him?"

I shrug my shoulders and stare down at my half-eaten sandwich.

"Look, Darryn, I've known Bryce and Derrick for a few years now. They are good guys. You have been here about a year now and not gone out once. Why don't you give him a chance?"

Well, so much for being the big brother. *Most brothers wouldn't be pushing you to go out with someone, they would be threatening to do bodily harm if they touched you,* I think to myself.

"Why do you keep on me about going out?"

"Because you are a young lady who needs to meet someone nice. You act like just because you have a daughter, your life is only about her. I believe your kid should be first, but you need a life, too, Darryn. You deserve to find someone to go out and have fun with," Tom explained.

Again, I find myself debating on telling Tom what has happened. Maybe then he would understand more of why I'm so hesitant. There is still a part of me scared that somehow my secret will get out. I can't afford that. It's more about Kendall than myself. I have to keep her safe.

"I'm just not sure if I'm ready to trust anyone yet," I explain, without giving the whole story. Maybe it will be enough to get Tom to stop pushing.

"Whatever that little girl's dad did to you, you can't use that to push away all men altogether. Not all men are jack-asses, Darryn. Plus, you need to look at it as his loss. That little girl is adorable. Now you can find her someone who would love to be her dad, and I promise you there is someone out there, be it Bryce or someone else, who will love the both of you. You just have to put yourself out there to find them." Tom crunches up his sandwich wrapper and shoves it into the bag.

Not all men are bad! I know this. I just haven't had many in my life that haven't been, as Tom calls them, "jackasses." My parents died in a car accident when I was two. My mom had no family and my dad's parents' health wasn't good enough to take care of me. I was pushed around from foster home to foster home most of my life. Most of the homes I was put into, the men either didn't have anything to do with the kids placed in the home, or they were abusive, mostly verbally. I couldn't wait until I was eighteen. I got a job and shared an apartment with a friend from high school and put myself through college to become a paramedic, with the help of student loans. I have been taking care of myself most of my life.

"Hey, come back to me." Tom's voice breaks through my thoughts.

"Sorry." I wrap the rest of my sandwich up and shove it in the bag, I'm no longer hungry.

"What's going on, Darryn? Why do I get the feeling there is more than you are telling me?" Tom asks, concern written all over his face.

"Like you said, bad relationships from the past. Let me tell you, those can really screw with you in the future. Let's just say my last relationship was not a good one." I know this may be opening a door for a lot of questions.

Nothing but silence. I look over at Tom and he is just sitting there staring at me, waiting for me to continue. No questions, just the chance if I want to open up and tell him more. I need to have someone to talk to, it's eating me up inside to have no one, but at the same time I'm just not ready.

It's more like a fear. Not that I can't trust Tom, I know if I told him anything it would stay between him and me, but I think I'm more afraid that if I start talking about him then somehow, someway, he will find me.

"I'm not going to push the issue with you on this, Darryn. Just know that if you need anyone to talk to, Heather and I are here for you," Tom offers.

"I know and you have no idea how much I appreciate your friendship, both of you. I'm glad I can call you both friends. I don't have any other friends here. One of these days I will probably take you up on that offer, but right now I'm just not ready," I explain, hoping he understands it's not because I don't trust him, just that I'm not ready.

A call comes over the radio, saved by the emergency. Sounds kind of warped I know, but it cuts this conversation off and I'm good with that.

It's been a very long day. I have the next two days off and I am ready for them. I've been on a four-day stretch, taking a day of overtime yesterday. All I want to do now is go pick up Kendall from daycare and go home and relax a little.

Walking into the building, Kendall spots me and runs. I kneel down and catch my little girl in my arms. "Mommy."

The guy and the relationship might have been disastrous, but this little girl is the angel that came out of it. I never thought someone could love another human this much. Kendall is my world and my saving grace. The only reason I think I'm here today is because of this little girl. The moment I found out I was pregnant I realized I had to think of someone else, that was what gave me the courage to leave and change my life completely.

"I'm so sorry, Carrie, I didn't mean to have to do this again." The last call we were called out to caused me to run an hour late picking up Kendall from daycare.

"Darryn, don't worry about it, I don't mind really." Carrie handed me Kendall's bag with an understanding smile.

I couldn't have found a better daycare than this one. It's small, Carrie and one other run the program here. It was what I could afford. When I first walked in I was a little worried, the building is a little run down, not a lot outside, but it's clean and Carrie is amazing with the kids, and my crazy schedule.

"I have no idea how I got so lucky to find you. I'm sorry I didn't call." By the time we cleaned up from the last call, I was already twenty minutes late on picking up Kendall. We pulled back into the office, I ran straight to my car and flew over here.

"Darryn, please stop worrying. You told us what you did for a living at the beginning. Trust me, I understand emergencies don't run on a schedule." Carrie spoke softly, then bent down to Kendall, "We will see you in a couple days, little one."

Kendall pulled away from me and gave Carrie a hug, then turned and raised her arms for me to pick her up.

"Thank you again, Carrie." Turning, I quickly walk out, not wanting to take up any more of her time with apologies. I'm sure she is just as ready to head home as I am.

I decided grabbing a small pizza on the way home for dinner would be better and quicker than trying to figure out what to cook, plus it's one of Kendall's favorites. Dinner, quick bath, a story and Kendall is asleep by 8:30 tonight.

I jump into a quick shower and with sweatpants and my favorite comfy t-shirt on, finally plop down on the couch and click on the television. The news is on, covering an accident on the freeway from earlier today. I am getting ready to change the channel when one of the police officers on the accident catches my attention in the background behind the reporter. It's Bryce! Actually, it could be either one of them. I can't really tell. Picking up my phone, I hit the button and the screen lights up. I open up the contacts and right on top under new contacts is Bryce's name and number staring back at me. He left it completely in my ball park to contact him. My thumb hovers over the call button. What would I say? Instead of pushing call, I turn the screen off, throwing the phone on the couch next to me. Now I'm just pissed at myself. I'm still letting him run my life.

"Darryn, we are good to go here. That guy we were just with signed the waiver to not accept transportation to the hospital." Tom comes up behind me with the gurney.

Quickly we clean up and secure everything back down. I round the rig and just about to jump into the passenger seat. "Darryn." I hear my name from behind me.

Turning around, I see Bryce walking toward me. It's been almost two weeks since I saw him at the hospital and he gave me his number. I turn to look at Tom in the driver's seat. He is sitting there, looking down at some paperwork on his clip-board, with a huge smile on his face. I turn my attention back to Bryce and find him now standing just a couple feet away from me.

"How are you?" Bryce asks. The smile he gives me almost causes my knees to buckle. I lean back against the passenger seat just in case.

"I'm good, how are you?" I ask back, wanting to turn

around and yell at Tom to stop smiling like I know he is right now.

"Good, thanks. Hey, Tom, how are things going with you? How's Heather doing?" Bryce surprises me when he asks how Heather is doing. I didn't know they knew each other that well.

"We are good. How is Charliee doing?" Tom asks in return.

"Good. I think we are all driving her crazy. It's hard for any of us to leave her alone since she has been home." Bryce laughs and I about melt to the ground.

"Understandable, happy to hear she is home and doing well."

Bryce looks back at me. "So I have now asked you out I don't remember how many times. I have given you my number, but you haven't called. Most guys would take that hint and leave you alone, I'm sure. I was going to, but I want to give it one more shot. So, Darryn, would you please allow me to take you and your little one out to dinner?"

One more shot! That's what he just said. This is going to be the last time he asks me out. I can tell him no and he won't ask me again. You would think that would make me happy to hear, but surprisingly it doesn't. I have to admit, I have liked all the playful times he has asked me out. What do I expect him to do, though, when I keep telling him no, or not answering at all? He will get tired of the game and just stop talking to me. I don't want that, I realize.

I hold my hand out to him. "Can I have your phone please?"

He doesn't even hesitate. I watch as he reaches into his pocket, pulling out his phone and puts it into my hand. I quickly type my name and number into his contacts and hand it back.

"I'm off tomorrow." Before I can change my mind and grab the phone back out of his hand and erase my number, I jump into the passenger seat and shut the door.

Tom is laughing next to me as he starts up the engine. "Shut up, Tom, or I will find something to throw at you."

"I can't believe you finally told him yes."

That makes two of us right now. I look out the window as we pull away and Bryce is walking back toward his car. Excitement and fear race through me together.

CHAPTER FOUR

Bryce

"I'm guessing from that smile on your face, she finally said yes." Derrick starts up the car as I shut the passenger door.

"She gave me her number and told me she is off tomorrow, so I'm going to take that as a yes." I want to call the number now and make sure it's hers and not a fake one to make me go away.

"Are you sure you want to get involved with someone who has a kid?" Derrick asks.

"Look, it's one date, I'm not marrying her. Kids don't scare me like they scare you." I'm starting to get a little annoyed with his constant questions about her having a kid.

"Calm down, man. I'm not trying to piss you off, just making sure you know what you could be getting yourself into, that's all," Derrick defends himself. "I don't have a problem with kids. I love kids, just don't think I'm ready for any right now."

"I don't know what it is about Darryn, but I want to get to know her more. Her being a mom doesn't change that at all," I reassure my brother.

"All right, well I will only say this then. I'm happy that she has finally stopped turning you down. It was getting a little embarrassing to keep watching it happen."

"Shut up."

The day felt like it dragged by. It wasn't real busy, which is a good thing in this profession, I know, but it makes for a long day in a car with my brother. We handed out a couple tickets, one small accident where we spent more time calming down both parties than we did writing the report. There was no visible damage to either car, but of course to both parties their car was totaled and it was the other's fault.

Before leaving, I put in for a day off tomorrow. I told the captain I had a last-minute change of plans and needed it off. He didn't ask any questions, just granted the time off and I left before anything could change.

Running through a drive thru for dinner on the way home and grabbing a quick shower, I finally sit down and realize it's after 9:00. Instead of calling, I decide to send a quick text.

**Is it too late to call you?

I am a little surprised at how fast she responds back.

**No, it's a good time.

I push the call button on the screen and listen as it rings. I'm surprised when the third ring goes off in my ear. Didn't she just tell me it was all right to call now?

"Hello." Her voice comes over the line. She sounds a little out of breath.

"Is this a bad time?" I ask

"No, not at all," she answers, but still sounds busy.

"Darryn, if you are busy you can call me back when you get a chance, it's not a problem."

"Really, it's all right, Bryce. After you text me, I had to run in and give a bedtime bear I forgot to put in bed and was reminded." She laughs, sounding a little nervous. "When I heard my phone ringing, I ran down the hall to answer it, sorry."

"Don't apologize, I just wanted you to know you could call me back if you were busy, I would have waited," I reassure her.

"I should be in the clear to talk right now, but can't make any promises." She is definitely nervous, I can hear it in her voice.

"So is it all right to ask what your daughter's name is, or too soon?" I ask, laughing, trying to put her at ease a little.

"Her name is Kendall. She is two. I'm sorry."

"Darryn, stop apologizing for everything." I'm not sure what she is even apologizing for.

Silence stretches over the phone. When I'm not asking her out, I have no idea what to talk about.

"What would you ladies like to do tomorrow? I have the day off, so we can plan a day out, or if you just have time for dinner, we can plan for that. You just tell me what you two like." I decide to skip the small talk and go straight to date conversation.

"Why don't we start off with either lunch or dinner?" Darryn suggests.

I sit here for a moment silently trying to figure out what we could do since we have a child with us. It's not like I can invite her out for a drink or anything.

"All right, I'm going to be very honest with you, Darryn. My experience with taking out a little one is very limited. What would you two like to do? You name a place and time and I will either pick you up or meet you there. Whichever makes you more comfortable." Why act like I know what I'm doing? Just being open and honest with her I figure is the best idea.

Again, silence. I am about to ask if she is still on the line when she finally speaks up. "How about we meet for pizza around 12:00? It's Kendall's favorite."

"A kid after my own heart. Pizza I'm good with. Would you like me to pick you guys up, or meet you there?"

"I think it's best if we just meet there." Darryn gives me the cross streets of the place, which I know well.

"Sounds like a date. I will see you two tomorrow. Have a good evening."

"See you tomorrow." Darryn quickly hangs up.

I could hear how nervous Darryn was on the phone. I was a little surprised she didn't tell me that she had changed her mind. I think I will be surprised even more if she doesn't call sometime tomorrow and cancel.

Walking into the pizza place we agreed to meet at, I look around and don't see Darryn. I've been waiting all morning for the call from her saying that she has changed her mind. Now that I'm here and don't see her, I'm wondering if she just brushed me off without a call. Looking down at my watch, I see it's only five past 12:00. Maybe I just need to give her a minute to get here.

"Are you waiting for us?" I hear from behind me.

Turning around, Darryn is standing there holding a little girl with the biggest green eyes, and dark curly hair. She instantly gives me a huge smile, holds her arms out and leans forward for me to take her from Darryn.

I don't want Darryn to feel uncomfortable, so I raise a questioning eye to her. I watch as she looks between her daughter and myself. She looks a little surprised. After a moment, she nods the all right to me and passes her into my arms.

"You must be Kendall," I say to her as she looks me straight in the eyes, the smile still huge on her chubby little cheeks.

"She never does that, she is usually pretty shy around new people, especially men," Darryn informs me.

The last part about, about her not trusting men, doesn't go unnoticed by me. Being in my profession, that statement sends an alert in my head. I know nothing about Darryn's past relationships or the father of this child, but words will tell you a lot.

"They say kids are a great judge of character," I make sure to point out to Darryn. I want her to trust me, give me a chance. I can see the fear and uncertainty in her eyes.

"They do? So you are saying just because my daughter thinks you're cute, I should trust you?" Darryn smiles and I feel my heart jump in my chest.

I look down at Kendall, who is just staring back up at me. "You think I'm cute, little one? I'm thinking that is your mom's thoughts and she is using you so that she doesn't have to admit it."

"You wish." Darryn walks past me and up to the hostess.

"Mommy thinks I'm cute," I whisper to Kendall, but loud enough that I know Mom heard me. Then I turn to follow Darryn and the hostess to our table.

Darryn wasn't kidding when she said pizza was Kendall's favorite food. I didn't know a two-year-old could put away that amount of food. From the amount on her face, it's safe to say she loved it.

"So how long have you been a paramedic?" I ask.

I haven't asked much through eating. I've let Darryn control the conversation. I'm hoping that now that we have sat here for a while and I have answered every question she has asked, she will be feeling a little more comfortable to open up to me.

"For about four years. I was one of those kids right out of high school that didn't know what I wanted to do, so I went and just took some prerequisites at a local junior college, finally deciding on paramedic," she explains, but she seems to be holding something back.

"So I'm going to guess something happened that led you to choose that line of work," I probe.

She shrugs her shoulders. "I'm not sure if it was any one thing really. I wasn't part of some bad accident and owe my life to a paramedic or anything like that, I just knew I wanted to help people. I've never been good with being inside all day, so I knew I didn't want to work in a hospital. I didn't want to run into a burning building, or go in with guns blazing, so fire-fighter and police officer was off the table. I pulled over one day for an ambulance to pass and it just hit me, that's what I want to do."

"Go in with guns blazing?" I'm laughing. I can't help it. "You make us sound like a western movie or something."

"Is that where you quit listening? You are such a guy. Hear what interests you only and ignore the rest of the conversation?" Darryn rolls her eyes.

"I heard the rest of what you said. It's just that part was pretty funny. Just for the record, we don't go into every situation with 'guns blazing.' I prefer to keep my gun holstered if I can," I explain.

I watch for a moment as the expression on her face changes. The easy, laid back look in her eyes is gone and I want to slap myself for that. I was only teasing with her. Her eyes move to my chest for a moment and then back to my eyes. What's she thinking?

"Do the vests you guys wear actually stop the bullet?" Darryn asks, her hand going up and waving in front of my chest.

I see the worry in her eyes. Her eyes actually speak more than she does. If you pay attention, they will tell a person a lot. "I'm not going to say it's 100% going to save my life, but it will definitely help, but nothing is guaranteed. Of course nothing is in life, right?"

"That doesn't scare you? You go to work every day not sure if you will come back."

"Darryn, your job can be considered just as dangerous. You put your life at risk every day you go to work as well. Don't get me wrong. Yes, I have a larger possibility with my job, but you can be called out to someone on drugs and he can have a needle you don't know about and stick you with it. You still do your job. It's all about helping someone in trouble. We don't do our jobs because we are worried about our safety, we do it because we live to help those in need." I watch as she looks over at her little girl.

I'm not a parent. Things may change a little when I have children and I have to think about a family when I go to work. Darryn is a single mom. I'm not sure if the father is in the picture, but she has to worry about what will happen to Kendall if something happened to her. I would think that would make her job very difficult.

"You are right. I guess I don't think of it like that."

"Will you now change your profession?" I asked.

Again, she looks over at Kendall, who is watching the kids in the booth next to us. "I know it might sound selfish but no, I can't change my profession."

"It's not selfish at all. If we didn't do what we do for a profession, people would die because they didn't get help. In the backs of our minds, yes we know what can happen, but it's our need to help others that drive us to go to work."

I want to change the subject, this one has gotten a little deep. "Okay! So what do I have to do to maybe convince you to take me up on an offer to head over to the beach for a little bit. It's a great day for a little sand play, maybe play on the playground there.

She is thinking about it. That's a good sign, she didn't say no right off. "If you have other plans, I understand and we can do it another day," I add quickly, wanting her to know if she does say no, I'm going to try for another day.

"No, we have nothing else planned for today, just hanging out at home," Darryn confesses.

"Why stay inside? I'm sure Kendall here would love some playground fun," I try to convince Darryn while I tickle Kendall on the belly, which makes her giggle.

"Bryce, why are you doing all of this?"

The question throws me off. What does she mean why am I doing this? What am I doing? "What is that supposed to mean? Why am I doing what? Am I making you uncomfortable? If so I'm very sorry, I had no intentions of that."

"No, I'm sorry." Darryn scoots out of the booth and quickly grabs Kendall out of the highchair.

I'm speechless, I have no idea what just happened or what I did to cause Darryn to just want to leave.

"Darryn, wait." I throw money down on the table and hurry after her.

As I run out the front door, I spot her quickly walking across to parking lot, heading to what I assume is her car. Kendall, being so innocent, spots me and is waving goodbye to me with a big smile on her face. The innocence of a child.

I catch up to them just as she opens the back door to a white Jeep Cherokee. "Darryn, stop and talk to me, please."

She completely ignores me and starts to open the driver door. My hand against the door, I stop her from opening it. "You need to tell me what just happened."

CHAPTER FIVE

Darryn

I'm scared! How the heck do I explain that to Bryce? He scares me, not physically, but emotionally. I watch him with Kendall and her reactions to him. It's all too perfect. No guy can be this good. I've been fooled by that kind of guy before. All sweet and fun. Says all the right things, makes you fall head over heels for them, then one day it begins, and slowly you realize you have fallen in love with a monster. Someone who wants to control your whole life, what you eat, wear, the friends you hang out with, the money you spend. I'm not going back to that. I'm going to control my life, not a man.

"Bryce, just let me go, please. This was all a mistake, I'm sorry." I try the door again, but he isn't moving.

"No, if I said something that bothered you or did something, please let me know." His hand stays firm on my door.

"It wasn't anything you did."

"Really? For some reason I don't believe that. Whatever it was has bothered you so much and put you in such a hurry to get away from me that you didn't even strap Kendall into her car seat. I'm pretty sure that's not a habit for you, so I'm going to ask again, what's wrong?"

I look into the back seat and Bryce is right. Kendall is sitting in her seat, not belted in. What the hell is wrong with me? I open her door and quickly belt her in. Shutting her door, I turn to find Bryce leaning against my door with one hip, his arms crossed over his chest, a questioning look on his face. He isn't going to let me go without an explanation.

"Listen, Darryn, if I did something, please tell me and I will leave you alone."

"It's nothing you did or said, Bryce. Kendall seems to love you. You have been great to talk to, very caring, very nice, but the nice guy act I have been fooled by before."

"Excuse me?! The nice guy act? Do you care to explain that for me?" Bryce is mad. I can see it in his eyes.

"Look, this is all coming out wrong. I can't explain it to you..."

"What can't you explain? Darryn, what are you not telling me?" Bryce interrupts me.

It's been almost three years! Three very long years of secrets! I never expected it to be so hard. Actually, only this last year has been hard. I've moved twice, and I really don't make friends. My last partner was all business, no fun, so it wasn't hard to not become friends with her. Tom is completely different. He is very friendly and so is his wife, I would say they are the first friends I have had in almost three years. Now there is Bryce, too. He deserves the truth, or at least someone who isn't living a life of secrets.

"Bryce, just take my word when I say this isn't going to work out." I stare up at him, pleading with him with my eyes to let it go.

He takes a step closer to me. His eyes turn to a hazy blue, and my stomach knots up. He's going to kiss me! I want to take a step back but my feet won't move. Placing my hand on his chest, I intend to push him away, but instead I end up clutching his shirt in my fist. His face moves in closer to mine. He stops just before our lips touch.

"Your words and your body are speaking very differently, Darryn." His warm breath rushes over my lips.

It takes everything I have in me not to pull his shirt that I'm clutching onto, so that the little space between our lips is no more. I hold my breath as I feel him lean forward and my eyes close. I wait to feel those lips on mine, but instead his lips move to my cheek. When he pulls away, my hand drops from his shirt.

"Thank you for the lunch, I had a great time. We will talk later." Bryce turns and just walks away.

I watch as he walks over to his car and gets in. He never looks back, and he doesn't wave as he drives past me. What just happened? My legs are still a little shaky and disappointment is heavy in my chest. I wanted him to kiss me. I had a death grip on his shirt, basically begging him to kiss me, after telling him nothing could happen between the two of us. After I basically accused him of putting on a nice front. What is wrong with me? Better question, what is wrong with him? I had turned him down many times before I finally agreed with going out with him today, and then today I treat him like a bad guy and he still tells me we will talk later. Of course, that could mean he will say hi when we see each other on a call or in the hospital.

Getting in my car, I sit here for a moment. I want to slap myself for the way I treated Bryce. He didn't deserve it. He was great today. He was fantastic with Kendall, and she likes him. She doesn't go to anyone. It took her forever to go to Tom and Heather. With Bryce she didn't even hesitate, she held her hands right out to him. This isn't right. I swore to myself I wouldn't allow him to control my life anymore. I made a pact with myself that I wouldn't stop living just because of the decisions I made. All of that is exactly what I have done today. I need to stop it.

Picking up my phone, I find Bryce's number and click on the text message icon. I need to apologize, tell him he was right. I want to see him again. My fingers sit over the letters to text it all out, I just can't get them to move. Throwing it on the seat next to me, I quickly start up the car and head for home.

Walking up the two flights of stairs to our apartment, my steps slow as I come up to our front door. It's open! My steps slow down some more and I mentally go through my actions as we left earlier. I remember walking out and shutting the door for sure. I remember locking the top bolt. Now I'm standing in front and I notice the door has been kicked in. Quickly, I pull my phone out of my pocket as I balance Kendall on my hip and hurry back down the short walkway to the stairs. I don't want to scare Kendall, but I'm starting to feel myself shake. My veins feel like ice is running through them. Without hesitation, I find Bryce's number and push call.

One ring, two rings. "Come on, Bryce, answer please."

Nothing, I get his voicemail. I try one more time, quickly pushing the call button once again. Again, his voicemail. Damn it, I quickly dial 911.

"911. What's your emergency?"

"I just got home and my front door has been kicked in, please send the police." I quickly tell the operator my address.

"Okay, we are sending out an officer, are you in the house?" she asks.

"No, we are back down in the parking lot."

"All right, officers are en route, I will wait with you on the phone until they get there. Did you see anyone in the house?"

"No, I didn't enter," I confirm and listen for the sirens.

It feels like it takes hours, but I know it was only maybe five minutes when I hear the sirens and shortly after, see two police cars fly into the apartment complex parking lot. The four officers run up to the apartment. A third patrol car pulls up next to the other two. The officer in the passenger seat runs out and up the stairs, the driver steps out and I recognize him instantly. "Derrick."

He turns and runs over to me. "Darryn, what are you doing here?"

"It's my apartment," I answer, pointing up in the direction of my apartment.

He heads up without another word. I just stand there and wait as they are all inside. I don't hear any commotion, so I hope that means whoever was here is no longer, but again they have been in there for quite some time now and my place isn't that big. What's going on? I watch as two officers come out and head down the other end of the walkway toward the other apartments. Why isn't anyone coming down and telling me what's going on?

The sound of tires skidding behind me has me turning around fast. I swear Bryce jumps out of the driver's seat before the car comes to a complete stop.

"Darryn, are you guys all right? What happened?" He runs up to me, his eyes searching Kendall and myself.

"Why didn't you answer my calls?!" I yell at him. I am angry and scared and taking it out on the only person here right now, Bryce.

Kendall starts to cry and puts her arms out to Bryce. He instantly takes her from me, which only seems to frustrate me more. I want to pull her back to me but her little arms are wrapped around his neck and he is rubbing her back, calming her down.

"I called you twice and you didn't answer!" I yell at him again, this time I can feel the tears starting to fall down my checks.

"I'm sorry," is all he says, but wraps his free arm around me and pulls me against his chest, now rubbing my back just like he rubbed Kendall's.

I take a couple deep breaths, breathing in Bryce, which seems to calm me quickly. My body begins to warm up, I feel safe in his arms.

"Darryn, why don't you and Kendall go and sit in my car, let me find out what's going on." Bryce pulls back from me slightly so that he can look at me.

He looks up over my head, I turn to see his brother walking back down the stairs and heading toward us. "I want to stay and hear what he has to say."

"Did you see anyone at all when you walked up, Darryn?" Derrick asks as he walks up to us.

Shaking my head, I try to think back to when I got here,

and when we walked up the stairs. I don't remember seeing anyone. "No, I'm sorry. I didn't notice anything wrong or out of place until I was walking up to my door and found it open. When I noticed it had been kicked open, I turned around and came back down here."

Derrick is writing everything down as I answer his question, nodding his head. "All right, well whoever it was isn't in there now. We have a couple guys walking around seeing if they can find anything, and we have contacted the apartment office to let them know they will need to repair the door frame."

I can feel Bryce's hand on my lower back. Strangely it helps, but unsettles me all at the same time. For the past three years, it's been me taking care of Kendall and myself. I haven't needed a man to lean on, but now that there is one to lean on, it feels nice.

"Darryn, while we are here finishing up, why don't you go inside and see if anything is missing so that we can put it in the report?" Derrick suggests and then turns and heads back to the stairs.

I start to follow after him when my name being called from behind stops me. "Ms. Carlsen, Ms. Carlsen."

Turning, I find our apartment manager running over to us. "Yes?"

The middle-aged apartment manager is breathing heavy when he reaches us. He puts his hand up to signal to give him a minute. He takes one deep breath and straightens up. "I'm sorry about the break in, first off. I just got off the phone with our property's handyman and he said he can come and put some sort of barrier up for the night, but will not be able to get the supplies to fix the door until tomorrow, so you might want to make arrangements to sleep somewhere else for the night."

Other arrangements for tonight? Where am I supposed to go? "There is no way he can fix it today?"

The manger shakes his head no. "Sorry, he is at the other site on some kind of plumbing emergency and says he won't be able to get supplies until morning. I'm very sorry."

"All right, thank you." I turn and head for the apartment.

I feel numb and I have a sick feeling in my stomach as I walk in the front door. It may sound strange but I was really hoping things would be missing out of the front room and stuff thrown all over. If it wasn't for the front door being broken, you would never know anything was wrong. I walk into my bedroom and that's where my breath catches. Papers are thrown everywhere. My drawers are all pulled out, the closet is all pulled apart. Nothing looks to be missing, which just confirms my worst fear.

A strong hand on my shoulder causes me to jump. "Hey, it's all right. I'm sorry, I didn't mean to scare you." Bryce's voice comes from behind me.

"I'm just a little jumpy, I'm sorry."

"Kendall is in the living room playing with some toys on the floor. Derrick is keeping an eye on her so she doesn't go out the door. Does anything seem to be missing?" Bryce comes around me and starts looking around, flipping the bed mattress back upright on the box springs, closing drawers.

"I don't have much someone would want to take. I'm sure whoever this was realized this after going through my room." I try to sound normal, but even I can hear my voice shake.

"This is the only room touched. Kendall's room is all good, I checked before I came in here." Bryce looks around. I watch, he is looking for something. "Where are you staying tonight?"

Shrugging, I try to smile. "Maybe I'll just go to a hotel or something."

"Don't you have a girlfriend you can ask or something?"

"No, I really don't have any friends here. Only person I talk to is Tom and his wife. They have a full house, though, so I don't want to bother them. It's no big deal. It should only be for one night." My stomach is all knotted up, what a way to end this day.

CHAPTER SIX

Bryce

Looking around the room and watching Darryn's reaction to everything, I realize something isn't adding up. She looks upset, but not surprised. Looking back at our conversation from earlier, and now all of this, Darryn isn't telling me something. I want to keep pushing her for some information, but I want her to feel comfortable enough with me to tell me without me asking. I need her to feel like she can trust me and open up.

"You two can stay with me tonight." I speak before really thinking. Derrick comes through the door at the same time, surprise written all over his face.

When I look at Darryn, the same surprise is in her eyes. A shirt she was holding in her hand drops to the floor. I watch as the surprise changes to a "really" look.

"Look, I have an extra bedroom at my place, you and Kendall can stay in there tonight. Why spend the money on a hotel? That's not going to be cheap."

Derrick's back is to Darryn, thank god, because the look he is giving me right now would have had her slapping the both of us and then throwing us out of her apartment. "Aren't you supposed to be watching Kendall in the living room?" I question him before he does something to embarrass both of us.

"I didn't leave her alone, I have a question for Darryn and then we will be heading out." He is laughing at me. He turns his attention to Darryn, "Is there anything else you need to add to the report as missing or anything?"

Darryn just shakes her head.

"All right then. Well, you know how to get a hold of us, or at least Bryce if you find anything else is missing or anything you think we need to know." Derrick turns back to me and nods, then he turns and leaves the room.

Darryn is over by her dresser, a piece of paper in her hands, and she is shaking. "What's that?"

Quickly she folds the paper and shoves it in her back pocket. "Nothing."

She is lying. She looks like she is ready to break down. I know all of this must be overwhelming but something just changed in her, a different kind of scared. What was on that paper?

"All right, Darryn, what's going on? You look like you just saw a ghost or something."

Her body is shaking and tears are forming in her eyes. "I'm just scared."

I walk over to her, half expecting her to push me away

when I wrap my arms around her, but I'm surprised when she wraps her arms around my waist and lets me hold her.

"Hey, it's going to be all right." I rub her back. "Darryn, look, why don't you and Kendall come and stay at my place tonight? I promise I'll behave myself. You don't need to be alone in a hotel with Kendall right now this upset. I would like to think we are friends and as a friend, I would like to help."

She takes a deep breath, her arms are tight around my waist. She fits perfectly against me; it feels good to hold her, it feels right. I feel her head nod against my chest. I push her back a little and look down at her.

"Is that a yes?"

She looks up at me and I see the tears are now flowing down her cheeks. I have to fight the urge to wipe them away.

"Yes, and thank you, Bryce."

"It's no problem. You gather some stuff up for the both of you and I'll go back out and watch Kendall until you are done. I have tomorrow off, too, so we will come back after they fix the door and I will help you finish cleaning up all of this stuff."

Darryn takes a step back, pulling out of my arms and I have to fight to not pull her back to me. She doesn't say anything else, she just starts gathering clothes. I walk out to the living room and find Derrick on the floor with Kendall.

"Thanks for watching her."

Derrick picks Kendall up off his lap and sits her on the floor next to him, telling her goodbye, then stands up. "It's no problem, is Darryn doing all right?"

"She's a little shaken, but that's to be expected. Who wouldn't be coming home to all of this?"

"So is she staying with you tonight?" he asks, sounding a little concerned.

I just nod. "Man, be careful, something isn't right here and

I know you know what I'm talking about. We have both been doing this job for a while now and we know the signs."

He is right, I can't argue with him on any of it. "I know what you are saying, I think the same thing, but whatever it is, I need to protect her and this little one," I point down at Kendall. "I'm hoping she will start trusting me and tell me what's going on."

Derrick stands there staring at me for a moment. He wants to say more, but he doesn't. "All right, well if you need me, you know where I'm at. I'll see you later." He turns and waves down at Kendall who is looking between the two of us. "I think she thought I was you."

We both watch as Kendall stands up and walks over to the two of us. She looks at Derrick and then over at me. You can see her little mind working around the fact that she is looking at two people who look exactly like each other. After going between the two of us for a moment, she looks at me and puts her arms up. "Up."

Picking her up, she wraps one little arm around my neck and with the other she waves to Derrick. "Bye."

Derrick laughs. "Bye, little one. I think she has us figured out." He turns and heads out of the apartment.

After making sure the door to Darryn's apartment is boarded up, we finally head back to my house, grabbing a quick something for dinner on the way. I pull into my driveway, Darryn parks next to me. Jumping out of my truck, I go around to Darryn's car and grab the bags she packed for Kendall and herself, while she gets Kendall.

"Bryce, are you sure this is all right?" She is standing next to her car looking scared to move.

I swear she is begging me with her eyes to tell her she really isn't welcome and she should leave.

"I wouldn't have offered if it was going to be a problem, Darryn."

With her bags in hand, I head to the front door. I unlock the front door and turn to let them in, but Darryn is still standing by her car. She looks scared.

"Darryn, if you feel more comfortable staying at a hotel, or somewhere else, you aren't going to hurt my feelings. I understand," I try to reassure her.

CHAPTER SEVEN

Darryn

W hat the hell is wrong with me? I haven't always been the type of woman who cowers from everything, always looking over my shoulder. I hate the person I have become in the last couple of years, I need to get back to myself. I know I can trust Bryce, he has been nice to me and Kendall, and was very generous offering for us to stay here tonight. I really didn't have the extra money for a hotel tonight, but I wasn't calling Tom and asking him if I could stay there either.

Walking up to the front door, I smile at Bryce. "I'm sorry, I think I'm still a little shaken up from this afternoon. I appreciate you offering for us to stay here, you didn't have to go out of your way today to help us and I know you have. I apologize for the way I have been acting."

"Darryn, I don't know too many people who wouldn't be shaken by what happened today. Just for the record, it's my job to do what I did today."

Disappointment soars through me when he says it is his job to do what he did today. I know we have only had the one date and all, and I have fought this attraction between us since the first time he asked me out, but him stating it was his job to help made me wish he would have done it just for us, not because the job called for it. What did I expect, though? I have done nothing but push him away.

"Well, thank you all the same," is all I can find to say, then walk past him into the house. I don't want him seeing the disappointment in my eyes.

Observing my surroundings as we walk in, I'm surprised at how clean and organized his house is. It is simple, nothing on the walls, a couch against one wall, a loveseat next to that with a coffee table in front of them. A big screen television with a game system and radio sitting below it on some shelves. Men and their games. It's set up as a large great room, the dining room and kitchen all attached. Carpet in the living room but wood tile floors through the rest.

"Follow me and I will show you to the spare room, it's down here." Bryce walks past me and I follow him down the hall.

The first door we come to is closed and the one across from it is where we go in. "Sorry, it's not much in the way of decorated."

I laugh. "Really, you think I'm worried about how your spare room is decorated?"

Bryce shrugs his shoulders and puts the bags down on the bed. "The bathroom is the next door down the hall. Clean towels are under the sink, if you need anything let me know.

The kitchen is yours to use as you need, please feel free to help yourself to anything in there. I will let you and Kendall get settled."

I watch as he walks out of the room and closes the door behind him. Kendall wiggles out of my arms. Once I sit her down on the floor, she runs to the door, opening it and yelling at Bryce. "Wait for me."

"Kendall, come on, leave Bryce alone," I call after her as I follow her out of the room. I find them both in the kitchen. Kendall is back up in Bryce's arms.

Kendall's trust of Bryce should tell me that he is the real thing. Actually, I should know that without my daughter's constant want to be held by him.

"I'm sorry, I think she has her first crush."

Bryce goes over to one of the cupboards and pulls out a bag of cookies. "Do you mind?" he asks.

I shake my head no.

"Why don't you go get settled and Kendall and I will sit here and have some cookies."

"Bryce, you don't have to take care of my daughter, she can come with me. You have already given us a place to stay for the night, you don't have to babysit as well."

I walk over to take Kendall from him, but she wraps her arms tightly around his neck and turns her face away from me. "Bryce."

"Darryn, she is fine, she isn't bothering me. I like having a little buddy to eat cookies with." He sits her down onto the counter and hands her a cookie, then he turns and offers one to me.

"Thank you." I take the cookie from him and lean up against the counter opposite of him.

Finally, Kendall is asleep. I think the cookies gave her a little sugar rush, it took two stories tonight to settle her down and get her to sleep. I change into my yoga pants and a t-shirt, and wrap my hair up in a messy bun, finally feeling relaxed for the first time today. Looking at my phone, I realize it's only a quarter after nine, and I know I should be exhausted, what with all the emotional roller coasters I have been on today—first time date, house being broken into and now staying the night at a guy's house I barely know. I feel like I should already be passed out next to my daughter, but I'm surprisingly very awake. I have already called work and asked for tomorrow off. They didn't even hesitate to give me the time off after I explained what happened. I don't want to risk waking Kendall, so I grab my tablet and head for the living room. Maybe if I read for a little while it will relax me enough to get some sleep.

Coming around the corner from the hallway to the living room, I find Bryce sitting on the couch with his phone in hand. He looks like he is texting someone.

"Sorry, I didn't know you were in here, I will leave you alone." I turn to head back to the room.

"Darryn, you don't have to stay in the room all night. Please, make yourself comfortable. I was just texting Charliee. I was supposed to go over tonight, but sent Derrick instead. I just wanted to check on her."

Great, because of my messed up life, Bryce is stuck taking care of us instead of his sister, who really needs him right now. "I'm sorry."

He looks up at me, puzzled. "What are you sorry for?"

"You should be with your sister, not having to deal with

house guests you weren't planning on having."

"Darryn, stop! If I didn't want to help, I wouldn't have. You needed a place to go and I have an extra room. Derrick doesn't mind going over to Charliee's tonight, that's what family is for."

I stand there for a moment and we stare at each other. He is getting frustrated with me, I can see it. "I'll head to bed, see you in the morning."

"Darryn, come on, stop hiding from me whenever you can. Come sit down. We can watch a movie, talk, or you can sit here and read and I'll leave you alone."

I'm not hiding from him, I just don't want to put him out in his own home. "Fine, what movie do you have in mind?"

I hear the front door open and my heart stops, he is home. Looking at the clock, it's after two in the morning. I was hoping he wouldn't be home tonight. Coming home this late means he is probably drunk. I make a quick mental note of the house, making sure everything is clean and put in place. Of course if he is drunk it won't matter, he will either find a reason to become outraged and he will take it out on me, or he will be wanting sex. Nothing pleasurable for me, all for him and only him. Jumping out of bed, I quickly undress, maybe I can at least teeter it more toward the sex and not the hitting. I rub my now rounding stomach, I need to protect this little one.

It's dark but I know the moment he enters the room, I can hear him stumble around. My stomach becomes nauseous as I hear his clothes hit the floor. I'm trying to keep my breathing even and not move. Maybe, just maybe he will just lay down and go to sleep. The bed dips and his arms snake around my waist. So much for just going to sleep. It is wishful thinking, it never happens that way.

He begins to grind into me from behind, his hand is on my stomach. I can feel his hot breath in my ear and I can smell the liquor on his breath as he begins to breathe heavier. I want to leave him, run to a place he can never find me, but like he reminds me every day, where will I go? I have no job, he made sure of that. I have no friends, again something he made sure of and no family. I have a baby on the way, how would I take care of the two of us?

"I have a secret." His voice brings me out of my own thoughts.

I don't respond, I have learned that he talks more if I stay quiet.

"You will never see this baby, Serina."

My eyes fly open and I sit straight up. Looking around, I have to remember where I am. The television is off and as I look to my right, I see Bryce. He is awake now as well, looking around. I must have startled him.

"What's wrong?"

I stand up quickly and look anywhere but at him. "Sorry, I think we fell asleep. When I woke, it took me a minute to remember where I was."

I'm a little afraid to turn and look at him, he will know there is more to it than just waking up in a strange place. I would put money on the fact that Bryce already knows more is going on than I am telling him, I think he is waiting for me to tell him first. I wish I could, everything is starting to weigh on me now, and with today happening I need to decide what I want to do. Run or stay and fight.

CHAPTER EIGHT

Bryce

Something is wrong, more than just not remembering where she is. She isn't looking at me, and is making a point not to. She is shaking and looking around like she needs an escape.

"Darryn, what's wrong?"

She doesn't look at me, she just stands there, her arms wrapped around herself. All right, I can't do this anymore. I can't keep acting like I believe her when she tells me nothing is wrong. Something is very wrong.

Standing up, I stand in front of her and close the space in between us so that she can't look anywhere other than at me. I'm standing so close that her crossed arms are against my chest. She looks down, that's the only place she can look. One hand under her chin, I bring her eyes up to look at me. Seeing the tears in her eyes, my chest tightens and it feels like someone is punching me in the gut. How has one woman affected me this quickly? I want to take her pain away. Destroy the reason that is creating those tears. I intended to question her, but I find myself wrapping my arms around her and pulling her into a hug instead. At first she goes very stiff, but I don't back away and after a few moments, her arms move around my waist, and that's when I realize she is crying. I feel her hands grab onto the back of my shirt like I am her lifeline, keeping her from drowning.

We don't move, I don't attempt to calm her down with words, I just hold her while she cries. I can feel the front of my shirt becoming wet as I tighten my arms around her. If this is what she needs, I am going to be here to give it to her.

Her shaking is starting to subside so I lean back to see if she is ready to talk. She still won't look up at me. I place my hand under her chin and tilt her face up to mine. My heart flips in my chest. Here Darryn is, red eyes and nose from crying, tears still falling down her cheeks, and she looks beautiful. I can't help myself, I need to feel her lips, and before I can really think about what I am doing, I bend down and claim her lips with mine.

It is a simple kiss, I taste the saltiness from her tears. I can feel her breathing against my lips as I look down at her. She is searching my eyes and before I can guess what she will do, her hand goes into my hair at the back of my head and she is up on tip-toes claiming my lips in a kiss that is anything but gentle. She isn't wearing a bra, I can feel her nipples harden and rub against my chest through our shirts. A little moan comes from her and I'm pretty sure just that little sound causes me to about lose myself. I kind of feel like a teenager getting kissed for the first time again. I need to stop this, she isn't in the right frame of mind and I don't want her mad at me for letting this happen. I am trying to get her to trust me, this isn't the right direction for that.

Gently I pull away from her, ending our kiss. "Darryn, we need to talk."

I watch as she goes from a dreamy look in her eyes to the realization of what just happened between the two of us. She tries to pull away from me but I'm not going to let her go and start closing up on me again.

"Darryn, I'm not letting you run and hide."

"Let me go, Bryce."

"No, you need to talk to me." I tighten my hands around her forearms and terror fills her eyes.

I instantly let go of her so quick, she stumbles back. She looks terrified of me. "Darryn, I'm sorry, I just want you to talk to me. I didn't mean to scare you."

She is physically shaking, her arms are wrapped around her middle, and she won't look at me. I know all of these signs, I see it more than I care to in my line of work. It confirms what I have been wondering about all day. Someone in her past was abusive to her. I'm pretty sure there is a lot more to the story, but I would bet my next paycheck that I'm correct about the abuse.

"Darryn." I take a step toward her.

Holding up a hand, she stops me but still won't look at me. "Don't touch me." She walks quickly past me and to the room she is staying in with Kendall.

It takes everything in me not to follow her and make her talk to me. Or to at least apologize for what just happened. The last thing I wanted to do was scare her away. I've been trying to get her to trust me, now I'll be lucky if she ever talks to me again.

For the past month, I have been asking her out. She always seemed strong, independent, not afraid to tell a man no. Then today it's been the complete opposite. She looks like she is ready to run and I'm not just talking about from me. This afternoon during lunch, things seemed off. She accused me of basically being fake, saying she had fallen for that before. That was my first clue that someone in her past had hurt her in some form. I wouldn't have said then it was abuse, but she had been hurt emotionally. I just figured she was worried about being hurt again. Now I'm pretty sure it goes way past just a bad relationship, and to top it off I would bet she is hiding from someone. Today at her apartment, she didn't seem surprised about the break in. She didn't seem relieved that nothing seemed to be missing. In my line of work we learn to read people, watch reactions, body language, facial expressions.

Ten minutes have passed since she went into the bedroom. I'm about to go and knock on the door, if for no other reason than to make sure she is all right, when she comes out of the room. She is carrying a sleeping Kendall in one arm and their bags in the other hand.

"Darryn, where are you going?"

She still won't look at me, this is becoming ridiculous. I grab her arm as she walks past me. Darryn freezes and I hear her sharp intake of breath. I almost let go, then think better of it. If she is ever going to trust me, I have to stop tip-toeing around her, so I hold onto her arm.

"Please let go of me?" she asks through clenched teeth.

"Not until you promise to stay and talk. You are running and you need to stop. It's after one in the morning, where do you think you are going?"

"Please let go of me," she says again, this time with a little anger in her voice.

That a girl, get mad. I can handle mad, it is a lot better than scared. She needs to be strong for herself and for Kendall.

"I'll let go if you promise to walk back into that room and stay until morning. You shouldn't be driving around town with a two-year-old by yourself this late at night. Where do you think you are going at this time of night?"

"What does it matter to you where we go?"

"Darryn, this is crazy. Come on, look, I really don't want the two of you driving around this late at night. If you are set on leaving then I will drive you to a hotel and make sure you are set for the night, at least that way I know you will be safe."

Something changes in her eyes. It isn't fear, or anger. It almost seems like a light bulb came on for her. She takes a deep breath and I feel her body relax under my touch.

"Fine, we will stay, but I'm going to bed." She moves to walk past me again, this time I release her arm and watch as she walks back down the hallway and into the room, shutting the door behind her.

I'm not going to push anything more for tonight. I'll talk to her in the morning, maybe after some sleep she will open up a little and let me help her.

My phone ringing is what wakes me what seems like only minutes after I finally fell asleep. Reaching over, I grab my phone off the nightstand. It is Derrick, no surprise there. What does surprise me is the time, it is after ten in the morning. I can't even remember the last time that I slept any later than maybe seven.

I tap the screen to answer and Derrick's voice comes through the phone before I can even say hi. "Hey, man, what are you doing?"

Rubbing my eyes, I fall back against my pillow. "Sleeping."

"Sleeping, it's after ten."

"What do you want, Derrick?"

"Man, you are grouchy this morning. Go back to sleep and call me later."

I don't even respond, I just hit the end button and throw the phone on the bed next to me. I don't hear any sounds through the house. I was expecting to hear some kind of movement. I'm pretty sure Kendall wouldn't sleep in this late. Knowing Darryn, she is keeping Kendall and herself in her room until I come out. She hates putting people out, so I can see her doing whatever she can to make sure I'm not disturbed by them. That gives me the energy to get out of bed. I think last night I was afraid that once Darryn thought I was asleep, she would try and sneak out of the house. I know one of the last times I looked at the time was about four thirty this morning. I must have fallen asleep shortly after that.

After a quick shower, I decide that I'm going to make some breakfast for us and then call the apartment manager to find out when the door to Darryn's apartment will be fixed. Walking up to the spare bedroom door, I knock and wait. Nothing, I don't hear any sounds coming from the room. Kendall is a two-year-old, it can't be easy to keep her quiet. I knock again and still nothing.

"Darryn, are you guys awake?"

I try the handle and it's not locked, opening the door I find an empty room. Darryn and Kendall are gone along with their bags. I go to the front door, opening it to see her car is no longer in the driveway. She left either while I was asleep or when I was in the shower. I pull my phone out of my pocket and look to see if she left any messages that I may have missed, but there is nothing. Finding her name in my contacts list, I hit send. It doesn't even ring, it goes straight to voicemail. I'm not going to even bother with leaving a message, if she left without telling me then she isn't going to call me back.

Frustrated, I don't know what to do anymore. Darryn obviously doesn't want my help, maybe I need to take the hints and just leave her alone. Shutting the door, I walk down the hall and into the living room, flopping down onto the couch. This is crazy, she is driving me crazy! I'm not one of those guys that can't take a hint. Sure, she turned me down a number of times when I asked her out. It was more a game between the two of us. She never acted disgusted that I was asking or insulted. She would have that playful gleam in her eyes. She finally says yes and the playful look is gone. On our date yesterday she seemed nervous, which I didn't take personally. Well, at least not until she accused me of being fake. Then at her apartment yesterday, she looked defeated, like she was ready to surrender over the fight.

Then last night when we kissed, something happened. The first kiss was soft, and with just that one touch of her lips it felt like something slammed into my chest, opening it to feelings I have never felt for a woman before. Then she claimed my lips in a kiss that shook me to my core. She held on like I was her security and all I wanted to do was wrap her in tighter and protect her from all that was making her run.

Now I sit here and know I should just let her go. She left without a word, she turned off her phone. How many clues do I need to know that she doesn't want to talk to me? I'm not going to beg her to accept my help, or me, no matter the feelings I'm having for her. There is another factor in all of this, Kendall! I love kids, I have always wanted a family with a few of them. Dating a girl with kids never bothered me, I just never dated one with any. Kendall's little arms around my neck and her head resting on my shoulder melted my heart. In a very short time these two ladies have wiggled their way into my life and my heart, how am I supposed to walk away from that?

Picking up my phone, I text her.

**I'm here if you need me.

I'm leaving it at that, I'm not chasing her, no matter how much I want to, but I want her to know I will be here if she needs someone. I really don't expect her to use it, but at least I know it's out there.

CHAPTER NINE

Darryn

It's been a week since the break in and I'm starting to think it was just a simple break in. Maybe they just got scared by something before anything could be taken. I don't have much to take anyway. I have nothing of value in the apartment, and the television in the living room is nothing to get excited over, it's small but it does the job. Nothing seems out of place, I haven't had any other problems. Sure, there was the letter I found, but rereading it I probably overreacted to it, going to the worst case scenario like always.

I haven't talked to Bryce at all in this past week either. We left around eight in the morning that day. His door to his room was shut, I took a chance that he was asleep and as quietly as possible left without bothering him. I was so embarrassed about throwing myself at him the night before. What he must think of me, I don't even want to try and imagine. One minute I'm all right, then mad, then scared and yelling. He must think I'm unstable, he would probably be right. In one day I accused him of being fake, and then yelled at him like he would hurt me, and then kissed him like some out of control woman. The man probably has whiplash from all of my mood swings that day. Then I turned my phone on later that day and his text popped up, telling me he was there if I needed him. Bryce was definitely someone special and I was letting him get away, but it was all for the best.

"Hey, are you listening to anything I have to say?" Tom's voice breaks through my thoughts.

"What?"

"That's what I thought." He rolls his eyes and takes a bite out of his sandwich.

"I'm sorry, I have a lot on my mind." I look down at my lunch that I haven't even touched.

"All right, what's going on? Everything all right at home? No more problems, right?"

I shake my head no.

"Good, because I'm still a little pissed at you for not calling me that day and letting me know what happened. Or asking for a place to stay the two nights you stayed at a hotel."

I called my complex manger after leaving Bryce's house and he assured me that the door would be fixed that day, but I still didn't go home that night. I decided to stay in a hotel for a night while I thought about what I was going to do. I didn't tell Tom that I stayed at Bryce's house the first night.

I was ready to leave altogether. I was going to go and grab our stuff and just start driving, like the last four times, but something stopped me. I can't say what it was but I couldn't leave. It might be because I'm getting tired of running, I'm tired of the person he has changed me into. I want my life back, I want to be able to think about having a life. How can I do that if I'm always running?

"Darryn, what is going on with you? All week you have been distant."

I take a deep breath, "I'm sorry, I guess this whole break in thing is affecting me a little more than I realize."

"You know we are here for you if you need us, right?"

I nod and smile up at him. Tom and his wife are a little of the reason I want to stay. I like having friends. I usually try and stay away from getting close to anyone because when I have to leave it makes it that much harder, but I fell in love with Tom and his family pretty fast. They left me no other choice.

"Let's change the subject, how are things going with Bryce?"

Not a better subject, I think to myself. "Nothing is going on with Bryce."

"Don't try and pull that blinder over my eyes. I saw the way he watched you yesterday while we were on that accident."

What is he talking about? Every time I looked at Bryce he was doing his job, I didn't think he was even aware I was there. "I think you were seeing things."

"Didn't you guys go out, how was it?"

"Yes, we went out for lunch, it was all right. We haven't talked since that day, though, so whatever you thought you saw, I think you were imagining it."

It was the only time this week we had a call together. Every time we are dropping off a patient at one of the hospitals, I swear I hold my breath until we leave. I'm always waiting to go around the corner and have him standing there.

When we rolled up onto the call yesterday, he was already there. My chest felt tight the whole time. I tried to not look in his direction but found I couldn't help myself. Kendall has said his name a couple times this week. How did he wiggle into our lives this quickly?

"Really, only one date? As many times as that man asked you out, I was pretty sure he was hooked on you. Men don't keep asking after being told no that many times unless they see something they really want."

"Well, I guess you were wrong. Can we please talk about something else?" I snap a little.

"Oh, I'm not wrong and that reaction confirms it."

A call coming over the radio has the two of us quickly putting our lunch away and getting on the road, saving me from anymore of Tom's questions.

Pulling into traffic, lights and sirens going, Tom looks over at me from the driver's seat. "This isn't the end of this conversation, just to warn you."

I don't even respond, I just turn my head and watch the city quickly pass by out of the passenger side window.

It has been a long day, and not enough calls for me. I know that makes me sound bad, but every time we pulled over to wait for the radio, Tom would start back up about Bryce. I thought guys didn't like girl talk. Pulling out of the driveway from work, I make my way to go pick up Kendall. All I want to do is get home, spend a little time with my little girl, and then maybe sit down with a book tonight. I love to read, just haven't made much time for it lately. It relaxes me to sink into a story that I can forget about my own story with.

I'm at a red light, getting ready to turn onto the street with the daycare when I look into my rear-view mirror and notice the same silver sports car that has been behind me since I left work is a couple cars back. The hair on my arms stands straight up. The daycare is only a little ways down the street once I turn. The light turns green and even though I'm in the right turn only lane, I go straight. The driver I cut in front of blares his horn telling me how "happy" he is about the fact that I can't follow traffic laws but at the moment, I don't care. My blood turns cold when I notice that the other car does the same thing.

I try not to panic, a person can't think straight when they are panicking. I try and talk to myself like we talk to patients when we are trying to calm them. It's not working, though, it's a little annoying actually. I need to remember that the next time we are talking to a patient. After a couple more random turns I realize my worst fear has come true, I'm being followed.

Reaching over to my bag on the passenger seat, I search for my cell phone inside. I need to stay calm. As long as I'm driving, I'm safe, right? Finally, my fingers find my phone. I hit the number I'm looking for.

"Hello." His voice comes over my speaker in my car.

"Bryce, I'm being followed!"

CHAPTER TEN

Bryce

When Darryn's name and picture flash on my phone, I am so shocked I probably answer it a little too fast.

"Bryce, I'm being followed!" Her voice is shaking.

I am just leaving work. I just left the building and was walking out to my car, now I am running. "What do you mean you are being followed? Where are you?"

"I was around the corner from Kendall's daycare when I noticed a car behind me that I had seen since I left work. Instead of turning, I went straight, I've made a couple random turns and the car is still there. I'm sorry, you were the first one I thought to call."

She sounds scared, but she isn't freaking out. She is doing everything right actually. "How far behind you is the car?"

"They usually stay about two cars behind, I'm not sure

how many more turns I can make before they figure out I know they are back there."

"Where are you exactly?"

She tells me her location and I realize she is headed straight to the station, good girl. "Keep coming this direction, Darryn. When you get here park on the curb next to the front door and go inside, I will meet you in there."

"Don't hang up, Bryce, talk to me until I get there," she pleads with me.

Her voice slams into my chest like a sledge hammer. I need to have her by me, in my arms so that I know she is all right. I need to stay calm for her. "I'm not hanging up, Darryn, I'm here with you. I'm always here for you!"

I hear her take a couple deep breaths over the phone. "Where are you now?"

"A block away. Bryce, I'm sorry."

I just walked back into the station when she says I'm sorry, I stumble back a little. This call shouldn't be affecting me like it is right now. This is my job, I'm supposed to be the calm one, but right now I feel like someone is tearing my heart out of my chest.

I was parked in the back of the building behind our locked gate and I quickly ran to the front. I come up to the front desk. "Darryn, describe the car to me." I tap on the desk to get the officer behind the desk's attention, "We need a car out front and ready to follow a car coming up to the station." I repeat the car's description that Darryn is giving me.

"They know where I'm headed. They just turned around, heading back in the direction we just came from. They just U-turned in the middle of the road."

I have Darryn on speaker and the officer sends the report over the radio to the officer waiting. I look up as the front doors open and Darryn comes running in, right into my arms, her head buried into my chest.

"Do I need to call for medical attention?" Carly, one of our female officers, asks.

I shake my head no. "I'm taking her to the breakroom, let me know if they find the car."

Darryn lets me lead her back, she is shaking. We walk inside and luckily, no one is in here. "Darryn, you need to call the daycare and let them know I'm coming to pick up Kendall."

She shakes her head no. "I'll go get her."

"After you calm down, you will leave with me. My car is parked out back, we will go and pick up Kendall, but you are staying in the car. Then we are going back to my place and you are going to tell me what the hell is going on."

I watch Darryn nod her head, but I hate the defeated look in her eyes. She isn't being given any choice on trusting me any longer. Being followed makes this a problem that I am no longer going to ignore or give her space on. She needs help regardless if she wants it or not, and I am going to help her if she wants me to or not.

Carly, the officer from the front desk, opens the door and motions for me to join her out in the hallway. "I'll be right back, then we will leave."

Again, Darryn just nods. She keeps her face down and her hands folded in her lap. I follow Carly out into the hall. "What's up?"

"They weren't able to find the vehicle."

It doesn't surprise me. I'm a little pissed at myself for not getting in here faster and getting a squad car out and headed in her direction sooner. I wanted to make sure Darryn was safe, keep her calm on the phone and get her to the station and out of danger.

"Thanks." I head back into the room with Darryn. "They weren't able to find the car."

"I should have gotten a plate number, but they stayed far enough back and with cars in between us, I never could see the plate or if it even had one."

"I need your apartment keys and a list of what you want an officer to pick up from your apartment for a couple days for you and Kendall. They will bring it back here to the station and I'll come back and pick it up tomorrow."

"What about for tonight?"

"I have sweats and a t-shirt you can borrow for the night, I don't have anything for Kendall, though."

"She has extra stuff and pajamas in her bag at daycare, I always tend to pack too much for her." She laughs a little, shrugging her shoulders.

I want to pull her into my arms and promise her every-thing is going to be all right. Let her know I am here and I'm not going to let anyone or anything hurt her or Kendall, but I need her to open up to me. She needs to tell me what is going on and all of it. I need to stay strong with her right now. She needs to know I'm not letting her run from me this time.

"Come on, let's go pick up Kendall."

Walking into the daycare, Kendall notices me right away, running over to me. I kneel down and catch her in my arms, standing up with her in my arms.

"You must be Bryce." A middle-aged woman holds her hand out to me. "I'm Carrie."

"It's nice to meet you. Sorry we are late getting this little one picked up tonight."

"It's no problem. Is everything all right? Darryn sounded different on the phone tonight."

I notice the real concern in Carrie's eyes. "Everything is good, thank you, though."

Carrie doesn't believe me and that is fine. I turn my attention to Kendall, tickling her on her side. "Are you ready to go?"

Carrie hands me her bag. "If Darryn needs anything, please tell her to call me."

"I will, thank you. She did tell me to tell you Kendall won't be here tomorrow, she took the day off."

Carrie just nods and smiles. I return the smile and turn to leave.

CHAPTER ELEVEN

Darryn

I watch as Bryce comes out of the little daycare with a smiling Kendall. I can't remember ever seeing her smile like she is. She likes Bryce, who could blame her, and Bryce is great with her. When he asked me out and found out I had a daughter, he went right into trying to do something that would include her. I wanted to believe there were men out there like him. Never thought I would actually find one. All I have done is fight him, from the moment he asked me out the first time, to the morning I snuck out of his house, and yet here he is helping me again. I have never felt as safe as I did that night in his arms. All I want right now is to be back in those arms.

The door behind me opens and my little girl's voice makes me smile. "Mommy."

Turning around, I turn on my best smile. I never want her

to know how unhappy and scared I am. "Hi, my angel. How was your day?"

She points at Bryce who is strapping her into her car seat. "Bryce."

I watch as he kisses her on the forehead before shutting her door and rounding the car to the driver's side. What the hell is wrong with me, why do I keep pushing this man away? "Thank you," I tell him as he settles back into the driver's seat.

He just nods. He's mad and I don't blame him. I sneak out of his house and never return his calls or texts, but the moment I'm in trouble I call him. Was I expecting him to be forgiving and happy to hear from me? Most men would tell me to go take a flying leap off a building, but Bryce can't, it's his job to help people and now he is stuck with us, at least for the night.

I watch him as we drive to his house. He is tense, always looking in his mirrors. I have now brought my problem into Bryce's life. I should have left last week, but no, I decided to stay because everything was a fluke. I should have known he would find me again, somehow he always does. Nothing is a fluke in my life, he has made sure of that.

I sit with Kendall and read to her until she falls asleep. Usually it is one book and then I leave the room, but I wasn't ready to face all of Bryce's questions yet. If I could get away with staying in here all night and reading I would, but I know if I stay too much longer he will come looking for me. He isn't letting the questions go without answers tonight, and I don't blame him.

I look down at my little girl. What kind of life am I giving her right now? Always moving, never making any friends. Sure right now it's not too important to her, she is too young, but when she is older she will start hating me for always pulling her away from her friends. Or one of these days, he is going to catch up with us. It's time I trusted someone.

Walking out to the living room, Bryce is sitting on the couch. "Is she asleep?"

Nodding, I sit across from him on the loveseat.

Bryce takes a couple of deep breaths. "Bryce, I know you are mad..." I speak first. I want him to know I'm not proud of what I have done.

"Darryn, I'm not mad," he interrupts me. "I'm frustrated. I have tried to be patient with you. I want you to trust me, to tell me what is going on. I didn't want to push you. You didn't really know me and I don't blame you for being careful. Then your apartment got broken into, you didn't seem surprised. You telling me I was faking being nice. The reaction you had after we kissed, or when I grabbed your arm that night. I know what all that means, but then today you have someone following you. I thought there may be more, now I know for sure there is more, much more, and I'm done being patient. Both of you are in danger and you are going to tell me everything so I can do everything I can to make sure you and Kendall are safe."

"Bryce, this isn't your fight," I try to argue.

There is that look again. The one that tells me he wants to grab me and shake me. I watch as he gets up from the couch and walks over to the window.

"Damn it, Darryn, tell me what the hell is going on." He turns on me and tries not to yell, I know he is trying not to wake Kendall.

I need help. I trust Bryce, if not for myself, then for

Kendall's sake. "His name is Brett Hammonds, he is my ex and Kendall's father."

I look up and he is standing there, no expression on his face, just waiting for me to continue. I might as well start from the beginning.

"We met while I was in college finishing up with my paramedic class. He had been persistent on asking me out. The paramedic class doesn't really allow much time for a social life, for a year the class pretty much owns you. I would explain that to him, and he would always tell me he would wait. It was very flattering. Some friends and I from class went out one night after graduation and Brett and some of his friends happened to be at the same club. He informed me that night I had no more excuses to say no when he asked me out yet again and he was right, I didn't. At least none that I could think of. Well, long story short we ended up dating. It's your typical story, everything was great at first, one of those too good to be true stories. He spoiled me like crazy and I was a young stupid woman thinking I had found my prince charming."

Now that I was talking it felt like it wasn't going to stop coming out of my mouth. I haven't told this to anyone, it's been my horror story to live, remember and run from. I can't bring myself look up at Bryce. I don't want to see the look on his face telling me I should have known better.

"One day I had received a call saying I got my first job, I was excited. He took me out to dinner to celebrate, we had a couple of drinks, went home and that night was the first time I saw the real side of Brett. I won't give you all the details, trust me, you don't want to hear them, it's your typical abusive relationship stuff. Before I knew what was happening, he had complete control of my life. My friends were gone, we did what he wanted to, when he wanted to and I didn't dare complain or suggest something or he took it out on me with his fist. Never where you could see the bruises. I even quit my job after only two months of working.

"When I became pregnant, I was surprised how happy Brett was, his parents were even more excited. On the plus side, the hitting stopped. Don't get me wrong, he found other ways to control me and hurt me. I'd always wondered how women could allow their lives to be controlled by a man, how they could allow themselves to be so weak and their confidence to be so low. Then, I became one of those women."

Now I know why I never told anyone this story, it's humiliating. Telling another person about the weakness you had to not be able to control your own life. Allowing someone to change you into someone you hated when you looked in the mirror.

CHAPTER TWELVE

Bryce

I t is taking everything in me to stay where I am standing. I
want to go to Darryn and wrap my arms around her. She
looks embarrassed and ashamed of what she is telling me
about herself. I want to let her know I don't see her as the
weak woman she is telling herself she is, but I need her to
finish telling me everything. If I go to her now, then most
likely she will stop talking.

"Darryn, why is he after you?"

"One night he came home really drunk, he kept telling me
he had a secret. I just laid there, I realized early on when he
came home that drunk if you just let him talk, he will tell you
just about anything. I just wasn't prepared for what he said
that night. He told me that I would never see my baby, he had
the plan all laid out. He never told me exactly what he had

planned, he just kept repeating that he wouldn't need me after our baby was born. That our child didn't need a mother who would raise it to be weak and useless."

I am waiting for the tears to start, but she never starts crying. That shows her strength right there, she doesn't see it, but she needs to.

"I laid there for a couple of hours running his words through my head. Something that night changed. I realized what was happening to me, I realized I didn't want my child growing up thinking I was weak, or anything like their father. I wasn't sure if we were having a boy or girl yet. I didn't want my son growing up treating women like his father did, or my little girl growing up thinking it's all right to let men treat her like he treated me. Brett didn't know it, but his words gave me the strength to leave. If he would have never said that stuff that night, I hate to think where Kendall and I would be today. I had some money saved in an account Brett didn't know about. I knew he was out cold for the night, a marching band could play through that room and he wouldn't have moved. I knew that was going to be the only time I would have to get away. I grabbed only what I thought I would need and I left. I waited outside of the bank until it opened, pulled out all of my money, closed the account and left town."

She is looking down at her hands, I need her to finish the story. If I am going to be able to help her, I need to know everything. "Where were you living at the time?"

"A small town in Colorado, I went to California first. When I got there, I had my name legally changed. It took a little time to get my paramedic stuff changed over, but as soon as I did I found a job. I played off not knowing I was pregnant, I was lucky the company was understanding."

"You legally changed your name?" I am surprised, most people wouldn't even think of that.

She nods. "Yeah, I figured it would be harder for him to find me if I changed it. I went with my mother's maiden name for a last name and changed my first name to Darryn. I met a girl with the name and spelling and loved it."

"What was your name before?"

She looks up at me, thinking. She needs to trust me and this is the test to see if she does. After all of the stuff she has told me so far, I am pretty sure the person following her today is her ex.

Darryn takes a deep breath and that's when I see the last wall fall away from her eyes. "Serina Alcove."

I think about it for a moment. She doesn't look like a Serina. Darryn fits her much better.

"For a while I thought he wasn't looking for me. When Kendall was about six months old, he showed up at my work. He was at the front desk one day asking for me, but he was still using my old name. How he found out where I was, I have no idea. I moved that night, giving the company I was working for an excuse of a family emergency that was making me have to move back to my parents'. I didn't want to leave on bad terms, I would need them for a reference later. Long story short, I moved to Minnesota, and then here. I thought we were good, until my apartment got broken into. It's him, he is looking for some kind of paperwork or pictures to confirm it is me, I believe that's the only reason my room was messed in. I don't keep anything out, I have a safe deposit box that has all my legal paperwork and pictures, believe it or not."

Now that I think about it, I didn't see any pictures in her apartment of Kendall. That should have been something I noticed. "So what are you going to do now?"

"I'm tired of always moving. I don't know what to do. I won't let him take Kendall from me. I don't want to spend my life running. I have friends here. Tom and his wife are the first friends I have had in years. I want Kendall to have a home. I want us to have a life, I want to stop fearing for my life. I save lives for a living, but I can't help myself."

There are the tears and I can no longer stand here. I go to her and pull her up and into my arms. She doesn't fight me, her arms go around my waist and she buries her face into my chest. We just stand here in the middle of my living room, her crying and my chest feeling like someone just punched me in it. That's when it hits me, I have completely fallen for Darryn and Kendall. Sure, it's my job to serve and protect, but this is different. The feelings I'm having right now are different. I don't want to arrest this man and have the system punish him, I want to find the guy and beat the shit out of him. Let him feel some of the pain that he put Darryn through, physically and mentally.

I give her a few moments, then sit her back from me so that I can look down at her. "Darryn, you no longer have to run. You not only have Tom here, you have me, and I will make sure Brett no longer harms you or gets anywhere near Kendall."

"This isn't your fight, Bryce."

The way she is looking up at me, her lips a little swollen from crying, her cheeks wet from tears, I have to fight the urge to bend down and kiss her.

"Are you supposed to work tomorrow?"

She nods.

"All right, well call in sick tomorrow, I'm calling in at the station. For now, why don't we get some sleep and then tomorrow we will figure some stuff out and how we are going to deal with all of this, but you aren't running, Darryn."

"I have nowhere else to go, Bryce. He knows where I live."

"Move in here with me then." The words are out before I even think about them. What surprises me isn't that I offered it without thinking about it, but the fact that if she says no, I know I will be disappointed.

Darryn, on the other hand, is very surprised by my offer, but she covers it quickly. "Bryce, that's very nice of you but for a couple of reasons, I would have to say no."

"What are those reasons?"

She pulls away from me and takes a couple steps back. "Well for one, this is my fight, not something you need to be dragged into. Second, after I left Brett I swore the next time I lived with a man, if I ever found one I could trust, I would be married. I did so many things wrong when it came to Brett, and even though Kendall is very young, I don't want to do anything that I wouldn't want her to do. I live my life now to show her how she needs to expect to be treated when she gets older. To understand she doesn't need anyone to take care of her, she needs to be able to take care of herself. Don't take this the wrong way, please, but we have been on one date and you are asking me to move in? That's seems a little fast if you ask me."

If the situation wasn't as serious as it is, I would have laughed. I understand what she is saying, after all that Darryn has been through, she wants to make sure her daughter doesn't make her same mistakes. "Then what is your plan?"

She shrugs her shoulders. She isn't running, I will do whatever I need to make sure of that. Not only because that is no way to live, but because I'm not going to lose her. I can't say

I believe in the whole love at first sight, but since the first time I met Darryn, I was taken by her.

"Why don't we get some sleep, clear your mind a little and we will figure this all out in the morning."

"That sounds like a good idea."

"This means you can't take off in the morning without a word, Darryn."

She gives me a shy smile and shrugs her shoulders again. "I really can't go far. I have no car, remember, we left it at the station."

"Something tells me that wouldn't stop you."

"True." She closes the space between us once again. Her hands go up onto my chest and then she shocks the hell out of me by stretching up and kissing me.

Her warm lips against mine is all it takes. I can't resist her any longer. My one hand goes into the hair at the back of her head and my other around her waist, pulling her tightly against me, deepening the kiss. Dipping her back down onto the couch, I hold my weight above her with one hand on the arm rest of the couch, one knee in between her thighs, my other foot still on the ground and with my other hand I grab her hips, thrusting her up against me. I expect her to push me away, but nothing could have prepared me for the feelings that shoot through me when I hear a soft moan escape from her instead. It almost undoes me all together. She has to feel how hard I am for her, with how tightly we are pressed together. Her hands slide up and under my shirt and it is like cold water being splashed all over me. We can't do this right now. I need her to trust me, not think the only reason I want her around is physical.

Pulling away from her is one of the hardest things I have ever done. Looking down at her dreamy and a little confused look almost has me saying screw being a gentleman, but if I want any chance of her staying, I need to prove to her that it is because I care for her and Kendall, not just because I am a man who wants only sex.

Standing up, I grab her hand and pull her up off the couch with me. If I look down at her laying there, I can't promise I would be able to go to bed alone tonight. "We need to get some sleep."

She just nods her head, but she won't look directly at me. She looks a little embarrassed. With a finger under her chin, I lift her chin up so that she has to look at me. I give her a small kiss and smile down at her. "Good night."

She doesn't say anything, just turns and heads to the room that she is sharing with Kendall. Once the door is shut, I flop down onto the couch, my head falling back. I take a couple deep breaths. That had to be one of the hardest things I have ever done. I would have liked to have her next to me all night, after spending some time inside of her, but it isn't the right time. I want to prove to her I don't want her only for her body, but for her heart as well.

CHAPTER THIRTEEN

Darryn

Shutting the door quietly, I don't want to wake Kendall. Leaning up against the door I take a couple deep breaths. What the hell has gotten into me? Something draws me to this man and it's kind of scary how I can't seem to control myself with him. Running my fingers over my lips, I can still feel his against mine. My fingers are still pulsing where I touched his stomach, skin to skin. He was warm and well built, I could feel his muscles flex under my fingers when I first touched him under his shirt. I can't remember ever wanting a guy as much as I wanted Bryce tonight. When he pulled away from me and stood up, I felt the cold air between us rush over my body, showing me how warm he had made me. Just thinking about it is making my legs shake. Sliding down the door, I sit down on the ground before my knees buckle under me. This is crazy, right? How can he be affecting me like this? We have had one date, how could I be having these feelings for a man I don't really know? If I'm being honest with myself, one of the reasons I don't want to run anymore is because of Bryce, but that doesn't mean I need to jump into bed with him, I scold myself.

Before Brett showed his true side to me, I thought I was in love with him. I can't say I'm in love with Bryce, but with the feelings I'm having around him, I can honestly say I wasn't in love with Brett, it was more like infatuation. I see that now. My heart skips a little every time I see Bryce. Even through this week when we weren't talking, when I spotted him at one of the calls we were both on, my chest tightened. Every time he smiles at Kendall, my heart feels like it flips over. When he kisses me, he makes me feel like I'm the only woman alive that can kiss him like that. He holds onto me tight, like he is afraid I'm going to disappear if he doesn't hold onto me tight enough. I feel needed, wanted, desired. I thought those were only feelings that happened in a movie or book, not in real life.

When he suggested I move in here with him, it took a lot to say no. No matter how I feel when we are together, or how great he is with Kendall, and how much she obviously likes him, I can't and won't go back on that one promise I made to myself when I left Brett. I stayed all that time with him because I didn't believe in myself enough to leave. I would listen to him when he told me that no other man would love me, that I wouldn't be able to take care of myself without him. The only way I can explain the feeling is like being under a spell. Like you have no control over your own body or mind. I knew he was wrong, but I couldn't say no to him or leave him, until that night when something just clicked.

Getting up off the floor, I walk over to the bed and sit

down next to Kendall. She is the most amazing thing that has ever happened in my life. I was given one amazing thing from Brett and that's this little girl. I want to hate the man, but I can't. He gave me this loving little gift, he gave me a reason to fight. Laying down, I stare at her. I smile just looking at her. Pushing a little piece of hair off her face, she moves a little, placing her little body up against mine. I will do anything I have to to keep her away from Brett, even if I have to leave Bryce and my feelings for him. She comes first, always.

Opening my eyes, I see the sun is up and shining through the window into the room. I reach over to the nightstand to grab my phone to check the time and that's when it hits me, Kendall. Flying out of bed, I look around the room, but she isn't in here. That's when I hear the voices coming from down the hall somewhere and her little giggle. I take a couple deep breaths trying to calm my heart back down as I listen to Bryce's deep voice and Kendall's higher-pitched but little voice. I didn't even hear her get out of bed. My ears perk up when I hear another voice, it is a woman's voice.

I don't even bother to check on how I look before I head out of the room, I just want to know who is here and why. Maybe it is one of the officers with news about Brett, maybe they found him. That would solve so many problems. Walking quickly down the hall, I find Bryce in the kitchen, at the stove, making what looks like pancakes. Kendall is sitting on a bar stool up at the counter and an older lady is sitting next to her. I've never seen this lady, and I'm pretty sure she isn't an officer.

"Good morning." I walk over and pick up Kendall, sit

down on the stool she was on and place her in my lap, kissing her on the top of the head.

"Pancakes, Mommy." Kendall points over at Bryce.

"Good morning, sleepy head," Bryce teases me, flipping a pancake onto the plate next to him on the counter. He points over at the woman next to me. "Mom, this is Darryn."

"Good morning, Darryn, I'm Karen."

His mom, my cheeks instantly warm. How must it look to her to have myself and my daughter here in the morning at her son's house? She wouldn't know I slept in the guest room. To top it off, I'm wearing Bryce's t-shirt and sweatpants.

"It's nice to meet you." I look at her only long enough to not be rude while talking to her and then look away. "What time is it?"

"It's almost ten." Bryce brings a plate over with a pancake all cut up and places it in front of Kendall, and then brings another over to me.

"Oh no, I haven't called work yet." I start to get up and go grab my phone but Bryce stops me.

"Don't worry, I already called in for you. I just told them there was a family emergency."

Part of me is relived he thought to make the call, another part is a little upset. I don't want work thinking I'm slacking with not calling earlier, so for that I'm thankful he called for me, but on the other hand I don't need him taking care of me.

"Don't give me that look, Darryn, I'm not trying to be in control." It's like he is reading my mind. "I knew you had a long day yesterday and I wanted you to get plenty of rest, that's the only reason I didn't wake you to make sure you called in early enough."

Well now I feel like an ass. I have to stop going straight to the worst, I should be thankful he thought about it at all. So instead, I try to play it off like I have no idea what he's talking about. "I'm not mad, Bryce, just surprised. Thank you."

"Yeah, right," he says and then turns back to the stove.

"Sorry if Kendall woke you up this morning." I'm really hoping she didn't go into his room and wake him this morning instead of waking me.

"She didn't wake me up, I was already up. She was talking away in the room, but I didn't hear anyone talking back. I knocked and she opened the door. I saw that you were still a sleep so I brought her out here with me. We watched a little cartoons and then came in here and started breakfast when my mom got here," he explains.

How the heck did I not hear her this morning if Bryce could hear her from the hallway? I'm not looking like the best mom in front of his mom this morning.

"Stop worrying and overthinking everything," he scolds me. How does he do that? How does he know everything I'm thinking?

"I pay attention," he answers my unasked questions again, laughing as he goes back and turns off the stove.

"So I have something to run by you. Hear me out before you say no," Bryce adds as he leans across the counter and steals a bite of Kendall's pancakes.

"Hey mine, Bryce." She giggles.

"Kendall, you can share," I correct her.

She looks at me and then her pancakes with a little pout on her face. After a moment, she looks up at Bryce with a smile. "I share."

"Thank you but I'm full." Bryce rubs his stomach.

My hand twitches remembering what that stomach felt like last night. *Damn, stop that,* I scold myself. "What do you want to run by me?"

"Well, we have a lot to talk about and figure out today, I asked my mom here if she wouldn't mind taking Kendall for the day so we can get things figured out. This way you won't have to worry about her at the daycare all day, and we don't have to worry about getting the things done that need to be done with her around. She needs to stay away from all of this."

He is talking in code. I understand what he is saying but I'm not sure about Kendall staying with a woman I don't even know, or that she knows for a matter of fact. "That's very nice of you, Mrs. Brooksman, but Kendall is shy, and I'm not sure how she would do with someone she doesn't know without me."

"Please, call me Karen." She puts her arms out to Kendall, who basically jumps out of my lap and into her arms to my surprise. "I don't mind at all keeping her for the day while you guys take care of everything. I love children and since I have no grandchildren of my own, I will have to borrow your child for now." She tickles Kendall on the tummy and she laughs.

My daughter is making me out to be a liar. She is usually shy and connected to me, but with this family she seems to not be bothered if I'm here or not. I look up at Bryce, he nods his head at me. He is right, she doesn't need to be towed around all day, or around any conversations that might be happening. She may only be two, but she is smart. "All right, if you are sure you don't mind, I would appreciate you taking her for the day."

Karen looks down at Kendall and claps her hands. "Then it's a play date. We are going to have so much fun today, little one."

I watch as Kendall claps her hands along with Karen. I have instantly fallen in love with his mother. Her eyes are so kind. She is the grandmother I always wished Kendall would have. Losing both of my parents, and with Brett's parents thinking their son was an angel, Kendall would never have any. I feel my eyes water up, but blink them back quickly. I don't need to make a scene that I am going to have to explain to this woman who probably already thinks of me as a mess anyway. I know I shouldn't be worried how Karen sees me, it's not like Bryce and I are in a relationship. Why do I think I need to impress her, or worry about how she thinks of me?

I look over at Bryce who is studying me. He shakes his head no at me. Why? He knows I'm upset and judging myself again, I see it written all over his face. He may not know exactly, but he has read enough through my eyes to see it. It's exciting and scary all at the same time to know this man has figured me out that quickly, yet there isn't one time that I can say that I have been able to do that about him.

"Well, I better go and get her dressed." I pick Kendall up off Karen's lap and quickly leave the kitchen before I make a complete fool of myself. I'm either going to cry or get up and round the counter to kiss Bryce, neither is something I want to do in front of his mom.

Walking down the hall, I hear his mom say, "Are you sure about this, Bryce?"

I stop for a moment, I need to hear what he has to say. What is she wondering if he is sure about? I'm sure he has told her about offering for us to move in, but I'm pretty sure I made myself pretty clear last night that I wouldn't be moving in. I expect him to try and change my mind today, but I'm standing strong on this one.

"Mom, I have known since the first day, even with all the hell going on that day, all the panic and worry over Charliee, I knew. So yes, I am sure."

That is cryptic. What has Bryce and his mom been talking

about this morning? Now I feel bad about eavesdropping. Here I thought she was talking about me and now I'm pretty sure I'm listening to a conversation I have no business being nosy about. Kendall starts singing at the top of her lungs, giving me away. I don't want to get caught standing in the hallway listening to a conversation I shouldn't be listening to, so I quickly run the rest of the way to the room.

CHAPTER FOURTEEN

Bryce

I hear Kendall in the hallway. Darryn is listening to our conversation, I'd put money on it. This isn't really the way I want her to hear about my idea. Moments later, the bedroom door closes.

"Bryce, if you are sure then you know your father and I will support you."

"Thanks, Mom, I knew you would."

"I just want you to make sure you aren't jumping into this without thinking it through. This is a lot to take on."

I know what my mom is saying, but I have been up all night thinking of nothing else. I need to make sure Darryn and Kendall are safe. I had called my mom this morning and asked if she could come over. We have always been close, my parents always made it easy for us to talk to them and be open.

They were smart about that, we never kept things from them and they never corrected us if we screwed up as long as we were open. We had to fall a couple times, but they would give us their opinion and then let us decide from there. She was doing that now.

"Mom, there is only so much the badge will allow, this will give me a little more room beyond the badge. Plus, if this doesn't work then I think she will run and I'll be honest, I don't want her to do that. I wish I could explain it to you, but there is something there and I don't want to let it go."

"Bryce, I love you and I will support you like I said, but maybe you should talk to Derrick as well."

I shake my head no. This is going to be very difficult to keep from Derrick, we always work things out together. That whole saying "two brains are better than one," we depend on each other for pretty much everything. I'm not sure if there has ever been a time I haven't talked to Derrick, but this is different. If he knew, he would go beyond the badge to help and I don't want him in that spot. I am going to talk to him about Darryn's ex, let him in on what is going on, I need his help along with Tom's, so this isn't going to be a secret for her to keep any longer, but this part of the plan isn't something I plan to bring anyone else into right now.

"No, Mom, just you and Dad need to know right now. Trust me, it will have to come out at some point because even after it's all over, I don't plan on letting her go."

Shutting the back door to my mom's car with Kendall all ready to go, Darryn is waving to her through the back window looking like she is going to cry. This is difficult for her, I know. She isn't used to trusting people and within a couple days she has had to learn to do it fast. I take her hand in mine, hoping to reassure her that everything is all right.

My mom rolls down her window. "Don't worry, Darryn, we are going to go do a little shopping, maybe stop by the park for a little while, have some lunch. You know, a little girl fun."

This is why I love my mom, she even knows Darryn is panicking and is trying to calm her down. I look over at Darryn who is smiling now at my mom.

"Thank you, Karen, for all of this."

"Don't thank me, honey. Like I said earlier, none of my children have graced me with any grandchildren yet so I'm excited about today." My mom looks over at me. "Let me know when you need us."

I just nod and wave as she pulls out of the driveway. I can feel Darryn looking at me with a questioning look. "Let's go inside and I will answer the questions flying through your head right now."

I don't let go of her hand as I lead her back to the house. Once inside, I figure there is no reason to not get everything out and in the open. I almost woke her up real early this morning when I made up my mind to talk to her, but I knew she needed sleep and talking to my mom this morning helped me realize I was doing the right thing.

Sitting us both down on the couch, I am surprised I'm not nervous. I am sure about what I'm going to ask Darryn, but I still expected to be nervous. Instead it just feels right. There are a few questions I need answered first.

"All right, so I have a few questions for you before we go into anything else."

Darryn just nods and waits.

"Darryn, where are your parents?" I start with.

"Um, they died when I was Kendall's age in a car accident. We were on our way home from visiting my mom's parents one night and it was raining. A lady hydroplaned, losing control of her car which went head on with us. My dad died instantly, my mom died later at the hospital. I had a broken leg and arm but other than that, I was fine."

My chest constricts, I can't imagine not having my parents, and thinking that Darryn could not have made it through that accident as well, that's something I can't and don't want to think about.

"So did your grandparents raise you then?"

"No. They were both old and unable to take care of themselves, they were in a nursing home together. My dad's parents died long before I was born. Neither of my parents had siblings so I was put into the system. Pushed around from home to home. Some weren't that bad, others were bad, only out for the money they received from homing a foster child. I'm sure you know what I mean. I was put into homes with so many other children and watched as so many of them took the wrong paths, or ran away, I decided I wasn't going to be like that. I stayed out of trouble and out of the way if I could. I tried to be invisible. Graduated high school and put myself through college to become a paramedic. I wanted to help people. I don't blame the emergency crew for my parents' deaths, but I wanted to be the person to help others if I could, save a life. You never know whose life you are changing when you work hard to save a life from ending."

I understand what she is saying, one of the reasons I became a police officer was to help save lives. My reasons just aren't as deep and personal as hers are. Hearing all of this just confirms how strong Darryn really is.

"I never expected myself to be one of those women I had been called out to help so many times. Unfortunately, more times than I would like to say, we couldn't save those who had gotten into relationships with the wrong person. I didn't want to admit I was one of those women. I told myself I would never let it get that bad with Brett, but it did. If I would have stayed, I'm not sure I would be alive today."

Hearing Darryn talk about Brett isn't helping my need to find the man and beat the hell out of him. I myself see a lot of abuse in my line of work and just knowing Darryn was in that kind of situation has me clutching my fist.

"You left, though. You got yourself away and your child."

"Sure, but look at where I am now. I can't even go home because he knows where that is. I'm going to spend my life running, moving Kendall all around, trying to stay one step ahead of Brett so that he doesn't get his hands on her. I won't let him anywhere near her. I will do whatever needs to be done to make sure that doesn't happen."

This is the time. "Marry me."

Darryn's eyes go wide, she even moves herself away from me a little more on the couch. "Excuse me?"

"Darryn, you have said it yourself, you don't want Kendall spending her life on the run. Never being able to make friends. It's not healthy for you either to always be looking over your shoulder waiting for Brett to find you again. What are you going to do, keep changing both of your names in hopes that one day he may give up? What happens if a day comes that you don't see him coming and you are alone, no one around to help keep Kendall and yourself safe? I know you are going to run, you don't see any other way around this right now. I see it in your eyes. I offered for you to move in here, I can keep you both safe while we find this guy. You said no, I understand that and your reasons, I don't want to force you into anything you aren't comfortable with, but I also know you don't want to leave. You are tired and it's understandable, no one should have to live in fear all the time and you definitely don't have to do it alone anymore, Darryn."

She gets up from the couch and starts pacing the living room. I watch her for a moment, giving her a minute to soak it all in. I watch as she goes through the emotions in her head, shock, denial, disbelief, back to shock, and then anger, that's the clue to step back into this conversation.

Getting up from the couch, I stop her pacing by getting in front of her and placing both hands on her arms. "Don't get mad at me, Darryn, I'm not trying to take control of you by marrying you."

Her eyes fly up at me, anger flaring. "How the hell do you do that? I think that scares me more than anything with you, Bryce. You answer everything I'm thinking, like you can read my mind or something. I don't have even a free thought around you."

I am going to have to tread around this carefully, choosing my words so that I don't piss her off even more and then have her run, because right now she is very close to doing just that.

"Darryn, anyone who pays attention to you would know exactly what you are thinking, your eyes say everything anyone would ever want to know if they just paid attention. I knew from our lunch together there was something you were hiding. If I wanted to know, I needed to pay attention. You were scared and I needed to know why. I don't want you scared of me, I want you to trust me. I'm sorry if you think I am trying to control you, I'm not. I understand everything you are telling me, even down to the reason why you won't move in unless you are married. I get it all, I swear. My job is to protect, but I can only do so much behind the badge. I want you to be able to give Kendall the type of life you want to give her. A place to grow up and call home and friends, but you know you can't do that if you are running and hiding. How free are you if you are running? That's not freedom, Darryn, that's letting Brett still control your life."

Shock, that's what shoots into her eyes and she takes another step back, keeping herself completely out of my reach. I don't make a move toward her, I want her to have the space to think.

"You think me marrying you is freedom?" she shoots at me.

"Darryn, it's not like I'm going to lock you up in the house. I want to help you and Kendall have a life without fear. You have to stop running." I have to take a different approach to this. I can't blurt out my feelings for her, she won't believe me right now. She would think I'm only saying things to get her to agree.

"Look, as soon as this is all over, you can divorce me and move anywhere you want to go and live the life you want and deserve."

CHAPTER FIFTEEN

Darryn

This morning when I woke up, I knew Bryce and I would have to talk. He offered for me to move in with him until Brett could be stopped. I expected the conversation to come up again today, but not in the form of a marriage proposal. I am having a hard time breathing, everything is moving way too fast, but what did I expect? This is my life. In a moment, it could change. Damn, why did I have to meet him now? Then again, when would have been a good time? My life is never going to be easy or mine if I am always running from Brett. Bryce is right, Brett is still in control of my life. He will always be unless I do something to change it, but is marrying a man I don't really know the answer to that? I'll admit, I have feelings for Bryce that I have never had for anyone else, but is it love? That I can't answer yet. I'm pretty sure marrying him isn't going to answer that question either. What other options do I have right now? Brett knows where I am, so it is either stay and fight, or run. I'm not only running from Brett this time. I am running from friends and Bryce. How long can I run? Bryce is right and I know it, one day Brett is going to catch up with me and I'm not going to see it coming. He will get to Kendall and how will I stop him alone? Then he would have Kendall and that alone is something I can't allow to happen. I swore I would do anything to keep her safe!

Taking a deep breath, I try to settle my nerves. I look up at Bryce who is standing there in front me giving me time to think it all out. He is even giving me an out after all of this is over. Oddly, that doesn't make me happy. A part of me, even when angry, was hoping he made the marriage proposal because he has some kind of feelings for me. He is offering me a divorce once it is all over; this proposal isn't because he has feelings, it's his way of protecting us. He is giving up his freedom to protect my daughter and me. He may not have deep feelings for me, but I think I just fell in love with this man.

Is what I am about to do fair to him? Taking over his life in order to keep my daughter safe? I know his job is to serve and protect, but I'm pretty sure this isn't in the job subscription. "Bryce, I can't let you sacrifice your life for our safety."

He takes one small step closer, close enough for him to cup my face with one hand. "Darryn, please let me help you. Let me help you get your life back, help keep you both safe. Marry me?"

He isn't demanding it, he is asking. I'm tired of running and I want to stay. Who knows where this will go, maybe our separate ways, but for now I'm going to take Bryce anyway I can. "All right."

"Really?" His hand falls from my face and his eyebrows raise in surprise. That makes two of us.

"You are right, Kendall is who I need to think about right now. I don't want her growing up on the run. How do I explain that anyway? I just have one request."

"What would that be?"

"We don't announce this to anyone. I don't want to have to explain why my marriage is for protection only." I don't want people to pity me.

"My mom and dad are the only ones who will know besides us. We will need witnesses so I had my mom come over this morning so I could talk to her."

His mom already knew! Great, what that woman must think of me. The conversation I heard in the hallway earlier is making complete sense right now. His mom questioned if he was sure this was the right thing to do. She didn't sound completely supportive, and I can't say I blame her.

"Stop that, Darryn, my mom isn't like that. I explained the situation to her this morning. Sure, she wants to make sure I'm doing this all for the right reasons and I wouldn't expect her not to ask, but she and my dad trust my decisions so they are supporting both of us."

"Damn it, Bryce, quit doing that, it's really starting to freak me out."

"What am I doing?"

"The whole answer my questions without me actually asking them thing. It's kind of freaky."

Bryce closes the space in between us, wrapping an arm around my waist, pulling our bodies together. His eyes turn that crystal color, it's the color they turn right before he kisses me. I'm not the only one with eyes that speak.

"Darryn, with this marriage I'm not going to push you. You can still sleep in the spare bedroom. I don't expect anything a married couple would be able to share, but right now I really want to kiss you," he basically whispers against my mouth.

Still sleep in the spare bedroom? He was marrying me to keep me safe so why did it disappoint me so much to hear I would still be in the spare room? What did I expect, to move into his house, into his bed? Right now, though, he is wanting to kiss me and waiting for me to answer him. How can I say no when he is this close? I know what those lips feel like against mine, it's a tease to have them so close and not quite feel them. My hand goes to the back of his head and brings his lips to mine. I hear his moan and my knees buckle. Bryce's arm tightens around my waist to keep me up on my feet. My other arm goes up and around his shoulders, holding myself close to him.

I can't seem to get close enough to this man. His body against mine elicits sensations I have never experienced and we have our clothes on. My walls are all down where this man is concerned and I'm going to have to be careful. This isn't a real marriage, this is a protection detail for him. I need to remember that.

Our lips part and he leans his forehead against mine. He is breathing hard, at least I'm not the only one affected by this kiss. I need some space from his body, his lips and the man in general.

"So what is the plan from here?" I ask, keeping my eyes closed. I don't want him to know exactly how affected I am by him. As long as he can't see my eyes, my thoughts stay to myself, right?

Bryce takes a deep breath and then a couple steps back. I take a deep breath myself and level my eyes to his, hopefully my eyes show calmness because my body feels anything but. Right now, all I want to do is throw myself back into his arms and claim his lips with mine. This is going to be a lot harder than I thought.

"I need to make a couple of phone calls. We need to get movers over to your apartment, figure out all of that. I need to talk to my brother, and you to Tom. I think it's time to tell him what's going on."

"I can't quit my job, Bryce." How can he even think to expect that of me?

"I'm not telling you to. If Tom knows what's going on then I will feel better about you being at work. I will know someone else is watching after you. Another thing I spoke to my mom about is Kendall and daycare. I want to keep her with family and friends while all of this is going on. I spoke to my mom and she was very excited to help, she would be more than happy to watch Kendall while we both work, and then on our days off she will be with us."

My head is starting to spin. There is so much changing and very quickly. "Speaking of Kendall, what do we tell her about us and your mom? What does she call your mom?"

"I'm leaving that up to you. She can call me Bryce, I know you don't want to confuse her with all of that. As for my mom, she can call her Karen or Grandma Karen, whatever you feel comfortable with. I had lots of moms and grandmothers growing up. If they were your friend's parents and grandparents, they were yours as well."

That's one thing I missed the most growing up. My mom's

parents didn't live long after my parents died, I was told. I had no family. I wasn't in one home long enough to make a best friend, or any friends for that matter, to call their parents anything. I stayed to myself, it was easier when I had to leave.

"I'm fine if she wants to call your mom Grandma Karen. Tom's wife has her call her Aunt Heather, so I see no harm in any of it."

"Next, we need to decide what you want to bring here from the apartment and what we need to put in storage for right now."

I think of our stuff at the apartment. The spare room is a nice size, plenty of room for Kendall's bed and dresser, I will just use the bed that is in there and bring my dresser in. The closet isn't huge but we will make it work. I'm getting a headache, this is all happening way too fast. I sit down on the couch and take a couple deep breaths, then ask the big question.

"When were you planning on the wedding?"

CHAPTER SIXTEEN

Bryce

When she plops down onto the couch, she looks defeated. I can only imagine what is going on in her head. Even though she thinks I can read her mind, there is still a lot of mystery behind those eyes and sighs.

I kneel down in front of her, placing my hands on her knees. "Darryn, take a couple deep breaths. We will get through all of this together, all right? Later this afternoon, I will call my parents and they will meet us over at the town hall for us to get married."

"Today?!" Her eyes fly wide open again.

I nod. "We can't wait on this. He is out there now, and you are staying here. Your stuff will be moved out of your apartment by tonight. I want to get Kendall's stuff here so that she has some familiar stuff around her, we don't want to stress her out. She is going to have enough changes."

"Are you for real?" She looks at me in disbelief.

"What?"

"Men like you don't happen outside of books and movies, Bryce. You are marrying someone you really don't know to keep them from a crazy ex. You worry so much about Kendall, you would think you were her father. You are turning your life upside down for us. Why?"

There is the famous question I have been waiting for her to ask. I can tell her it's because I have fallen in love with her and Kendall has taken my heart as well. That if anything happened to either one of them I wouldn't stop until I killed the man that hurt them. I actually wonder how she doesn't already know all of this, but I know she isn't ready to hear it from me.

"I promised you I would help at any cost so that you didn't have to run anymore, to give Kendall the life you want her to have. Let's think of it as a witness protection detail. Going undercover. Whatever you want to call it. I will make sure you don't have to look over your shoulder for the rest of your life, running."

I watch as she studies my eyes. There are tears in hers. She leans forward and kisses me softly on the lips. "Thank you, Bryce, for everything. I don't deserve someone in my life like you."

"You are so wrong, Darryn, and I plan to prove it to you." Leaning forward, I place one more kiss on her lips but know if I don't end it there, it may go further than it should right now.

Darryn is in the living room talking to the movers on the

phone, I need to call Derrick. I have never kept anything from my brother, we tell each other everything. Well, that's important anyway. Not telling him that I am getting married today is going to be hard, even before Darryn asked me not to tell anyone I had decided not to say anything to anyone else other than my parents. I need her to trust me even if it means me keeping this from Derrick.

Sitting on my bed, I dial up my brother's number. I called in earlier today for the day off, but he is on shift today. I'm hoping he isn't on a call right now.

"Hey, man, what the hell is going on?" Derrick answers the phone.

"I'm guessing you talked to someone at the station." I figured he would have heard about last night the moment he got to the station today.

"To someone, no! The whole station was talking about it this morning. Do you know how stupid it looks when your partner and twin brother has no idea what they are talking about? Why the hell didn't you call me last night and tell me what was going on?"

If Derrick is this mad about me not calling about last night events, he will be a lot of fun when he does find out I got married without him knowing.

"Look, it was kind of a crazy night, we had a lot to deal with and are still dealing with. If you can talk for a minute, I'll give you a heads up on what's going on."

"Talk fast because you know how the calls go, it's like they know it's not a good time."

I laugh, that is very true, you can go all day without a call and as soon as you think you have a moment, the city goes crazy. I quickly fill him in on the events from last night.

"Leave it to you to find a girl with a crazy ex. So what are your plans? Obviously she can't stay at her place without protection."

"Well, I guess you can say I'm going to be her protection, she and her daughter are moving into my spare room until this is done."

I'm not going to talk about the marrying her part, but I know he would find out about her living here so I might as well tell him now.

Silence stretches out on the line. "Derrick?"

"Yeah, I'm here. Are you sure this is the right move? Couldn't we put her in a safe house or something? You are talking about moving in not only a girl, but her daughter, too."

"I need to make sure they are safe, I can assure that if they are here."

"You really like this girl, don't you?"

"I can't explain it, something about her has just stuck with me, and her little girl is amazing. I'm not going to lie to you, Derrick, I've fallen hard for this one and I'm going to do whatever I need to do to make sure they are safe."

"Well, you know I have your back, but you need to keep me in the loop on what's going on. I don't want to hear about it from the station."

I expected a little more from him about the girls being here, it surprises me how easy he let me off about it all, but I'm not going to ask questions.

"Why do I feel like you aren't telling me something?" Derrick's voice breaks through my thoughts.

Why, because I'm keeping a secret about one of the biggest events of my life and it's driving me crazy, I think to myself. Derrick will forgive me, it might take some time, but he will forgive me. If Darryn finds out I said anything, she may leave and that's a risk I can't take.

"I've told you everything there is. I will be back tomorrow so I'll file my side of the report then. We sent out an officer last night when Darryn called, but they didn't find the car, so we don't have much to run on right now but a description of it. Can't really go after the guy yet without some proof it's him. Darryn didn't get a good look at the driver, and no one saw anyone in her apartment. None of the security cameras picked up on the face of the guy, he kept it hidden, so we really don't have much to go off of."

"Definitely not the ideal case. Just let me know what you need help with."

"One thing, I don't want Charliee knowing about any of this. Mom and Dad know, Mom is going to start keeping Kendall on the days we are both working. Charliee needs to worry about healing, not worrying about all of this."

Charliee has been out of the hospital for a while but she needs to worry about herself, not all of this, and she is the one who will worry the most. She has dealt with enough in the past month or so, she needs no involvement in this. We almost lost her once, I will not put her into the middle of anything that may put her in danger again.

"I agree, but you know when she finds out you have your girlfriend, much less a girlfriend with a daughter, living with you and she is the only one who doesn't know about it, she is going to be pissed. You know she hates being left out."

"Darryn's not my girlfriend." It's not a lie at least.

"Whatever you want to call her, be prepared for the wrath of Charliee when she finds out."

Wrath of Charliee, wrath of Derrick, damn the things we do for the people we love. I need to get off the phone before I break down and tell Derrick everything. I never realized it would be this hard to keep something from my siblings.

"Hey, I need to get going, I'll see you tomorrow."

"All right, call me if you need anything." Derrick ends the call.

I sit here for a moment. I'm not nervous about marrying Darryn today, something just tells me it is right, but what if she doesn't want this after everything is over? When I think about marriage, I think about sharing a life with a woman I love. Creating a home together, a family. Sharing my bed, my life, and our ups and downs together. Today, I'm getting married and coming home to an empty bed, a secret love for the woman and child, and no future plans. To top it off, I'm keeping a very large secret from half of my immediate family. For the first time I'm wondering if it's all worth it.

A soft knock on my door brings me back. "Come in."

Darryn opens the door and stands in the doorway. My breath catches like it does every time I see her, and like it has every time since the first time I saw her. She has absolutely no idea what kind of control she has over me. Is it all worth it? Most definitely!

CHAPTER SEVENTEEN

Darryn

I don't know if I should bother Bryce, I know he is in his room making some phone calls, but he told me to let him know when I was done with the movers. On top of that, I called Tom and told him everything. Well, at least the short version of everything. He promised me a good scolding when I get back to work tomorrow. When I open the door to Bryce's room, I almost stumble back. There he is sitting on the edge of his very large king-sized bed, leaning down with his arms on his legs looking defeated. It is only a second, his expression changes fast, but I still noticed it. What am I expecting from him? He is being forced to marry to keep someone safe from their psycho ex. Who wouldn't be happy about that?

"Sorry, I didn't mean to interrupt. Movers are all set, I even called Tom and told him what's going on. I figured you wouldn't let me go back to work until I did." I laugh, trying to lighten up the mood in the room.

He doesn't laugh, he just stares. I can't read anything in his eyes. Standing here, I don't know what to do. "Well, you just asked me to let you know when I finished on the phone, so I'll just be out in the living room when you are ready."

I turn to walk away. "Darryn."

I turn back to find him now standing right in front of me, I didn't even hear him get up from the bed. Before I know what is happening, he hooks a hand behind my head, claiming my lips. My knees buckle, he turns us, my back now against the door frame which is serving to keep me standing, with his body pressed tight against mine. This kiss isn't soft, it is raw. His tongue instantly finds mine, one of us moans, I'm not sure who, maybe it's both of us. His leg is pressed between my thighs and I can't stop myself from pressing my hips into his, my center instantly heating up. I can feel his hardness against me. I have never wanted a man as much as I want Bryce at this moment. His kisses aren't gentle, not this time. Usually when he kisses me I feel like he is holding back, afraid to break me. He is gentle, in control, but not this time. My hands go under his shirt and contact with his skin. This time I know the moan that fills the room is from me. My hands have been aching to touch him again since the other night. My hands tingle every time I think about the last time I touched him.

He stills the moment I touch him. He doesn't pull back, he just stops kissing me, breathing hard against my lips. "I'm so sorry, Darryn, I need to control this impulse around you."

No, no you don't! I want to yell at him. I want to take his lips back and finish what we started. Then something clicks inside of me. More like I came out of the trance he puts me in every time he kisses me. I want him, no question in my mind, but we don't need to complicate the situation by becoming physical with each other.

I can't speak, all I can do is nod. Bryce takes one deep breath and then pushes himself away from me using the frame of the door behind me. A chill runs over me the second his body leaves mine. It is so intense, it takes everything in me not to grab him by the shirt and pull him back to me.

"We need to get going," Bryce says as he walks away from me and down the hall.

The drive over to city hall is quiet. Bryce's parents are meeting us there with Kendall. My hands are shaking in my lap. I can't believe I'm on the way to get married right now. If someone would have told me even this morning when I woke up that I would be marrying Bryce, I would have laughed in their face. I guess this isn't a real marriage though, right? Sure, we will say our vows, be pronounced husband and wife, but there will be no rings, sleeping in separate rooms, basically in name only. Probably a divorce in a couple months at the most.

Bryce grabs my hand and I jump. "Are you all right?" he asks.

"Yes, sorry. I was thinking, you just surprised me is all." He hasn't said a word to me since we left his house.

"Darryn, I'm sorry about earlier. I don't want you to get the wrong idea."

In other words, he doesn't want me to think he wants me, I think to myself. Why would he want to get any more involved with me than he already is?

"Bryce, don't worry about it, it's fine. I'm really sorry about all of this. You have no idea how much I appreciate everything you are doing for me, including giving up your freedom."

"Stop, Darryn! For one, I'm not giving up my freedom. I have told you I will do anything to make sure Kendall and you are safe. Remember, I'm the one who asked you to marry me." He smiles over at me.

I can feel the tension between us start to melt. My shoulders relax, and my body warms by just him holding my hand. I'm waiting for him to move his hand but he doesn't, we drive the rest of the way, our fingers tightly entwined. This may not be a real marriage, but we are both still very nervous. Who wouldn't be on their wedding day?

Pulling into the parking lot, Bryce finds a spot quickly and turns the car off. I start to get out but he stops me.

"Darryn, I know every girl dreams of a big wedding, family and friends there to help celebrate two lives becoming one, I'm sorry this isn't going to be like that."

He looks upset for me which tugs at my heart. He is worried he isn't giving me the wedding of my dreams. That gesture does it, the last wall is down. This man may never know it, but he has my heart completely.

"I guess it's a good thing I didn't grow up like most girls then. I have no family or friends, well, maybe Tom and Heather, but other than that no one else." I laugh, trying to lighten the mood, but instead I see pain shoot across his eyes. Pain for a little girl who had nothing growing up.

I place my hand against his cheek. "Don't look at me that way, please. Don't feel sorry for me. I don't want people to feel sorry for me, that's why I don't tell many people about my past. Sure, I was passed around, and there were homes that weren't that great, but there were a few that were good."

Taking my hand, he kisses my palm. "Sorry. I'm glad you told me."

"I'll be honest, it felt good to talk about it finally, about all of it. You are an amazing man, Bryce, I just wish my life wasn't so screwed up."

We sit here staring at each other for a few moments. I wish I knew what he was thinking about, it's like he is wanting to tell me something, but instead he gives me a smile and then gets out of the car. I take a deep breath, this is it, it's time to go and become Mrs. Bryce Brooksman.

Bryce's mom and a man I assume is his father are already here and waiting for us when we walk up.

"Mommy, Bryce." Kendall's little voice echoes through the building when she spots us.

She wiggles out of Karen's arms and runs right into mine. "Hello, my angel. I've missed you today. Were you a good girl?"

Kendall nods her little head up and down, I look over to Karen for confirmation.

"We had a blast today. She may be a little hyped up, there was ice cream and candy involved with today's activities," Karen explains.

"Bryce." Kendall leans toward him with her arms out, signaling for him to take her.

"How's my girl?" Bryce takes her from my arms and gives her a raspberry kiss on her cheek. My heart melts watching the two of them interact.

Karen walks up and hands Bryce a box. "Everything is in here that you asked for."

I won't lie, my curiosity piques. Bryce looks over at me as his mom hands him the box, a small smile on his face. Damn it, he caught me being nosey.

"Darryn, this is my dad, Steven. Dad, this is Darryn." Bryce makes the introduction.

Nothing like meeting your father-in-law on the day of your wedding. "Mr. Brooksman, it's nice to meet you."

"Please call me Steven, or anything else other than Mr. Brooksman." He smiles at me and then winks.

I get his meaning, what I like is he didn't come right out and say I could call him Dad, but I picked up on the meaning of his words. "It's nice to meet you, Steven." I'm not ready for the Dad title yet.

"Come on, we need to get going, we have our appointment in fifteen minutes." Bryce takes my hand, still holding Kendall in the other arm, along with the box in hand.

It is strange, here I am standing in front of a man I have only really been on one date with, his parents and my little girl, along with the judge as he speaks the words that will marry us. It is like being in a tunnel, everything seems kind of far away. I answer and repeat when I am instructed to, feeling like I am in some kind of trance.

"Bryce, do you have the rings?" I hear the judge ask.

My cheeks begin to burn from embarrassment. How do we explain that there isn't any rings?

My embarrassment quickly turns to shock when Bryce speaks up. "Yes, sir."

My eyes fly wide open, looking at Bryce puzzled. He got me a ring? Why didn't he say anything? I would have gotten him one. How, I'm not sure, I haven't been out of his sight since last night, but all the same. I watch as he opens the box he has been holding the whole time. He pulls out three chains.

"Darryn, I know you wanted to keep this marriage between us." My eyes shoot over to the judge and my cheeks heat up again, what that man must think about all of this.

"Even as untraditional as all of this is, I couldn't let this one tradition go. So I bought us both rings and placed them on chains. This way we can wear them, but not in sight for everyone to question."

Bryce places my necklace around my neck as he repeats the vows the judge is reciting and then hands me the one meant for him. The bands are simple white gold bands, but the meaning behind them moves me to tears. I don't try to stop them from falling as I repeat my vows and place the thicker chain around his neck.

I look down at his hand and see the third necklace. A much smaller chain with a little silver heart.

"Judge, if you don't mind, before we continue." Bryce points over at Kendall who Karen is holding.

"Of course." The judge smiles at Bryce.

Karen puts Kendall down and when Bryce bends down, Kendall walks over to him. "Kendall, I promise to protect you and your mommy with my life and to cherish you both." He spoke to her like a little adult, as though she is understanding it all. She may not be but I am fully understanding it.

Kendall looks down at the little necklace and smiles. "Mine?" She looks up at Bryce.

"Yes, little one, yours. Now and forever," Bryce answers, not only to her, but to me as well. His eyes don't leave mine as he speaks to her.

I have already admitted to myself that I am falling in love with Bryce, but if I had any doubts about it, this scene I am watching right now would have sealed the deal.

"I pronounce you man and wife, you may kiss your bride." The judge finishes the ceremony.

Bryce places his hands on each side of my face and claims my lips. It is soft, one of those kisses that make you want to curl up against him and stay forever. One that says I will be safe at any cost to him. Guilt washes through me once again. He is putting his life and his family's lives in danger for me. What have I just agreed to do? This is so selfish of me to do to Bryce, he should be out living his life, finding someone who could give him a normal family, not babysitting me and my daughter. Our kiss ends and I bury my face into his chest. Yes, I am crying. There is no way I'm ever going to be able to pay him back for all of this.

"Congratulations to the both of you," the judge says.

I feel Bryce extend his arm out to shake the judge's hand. "Thank you, sir." He starts rubbing my back, trying to sooth me.

I need to snap out of this. It happened, we are married. I need from this point on to make sure nothing happens to this family and to make sure Bryce doesn't regret all of this. When the time comes, no matter what my heart is feeling, I will let him go.

Walking out of the building, the sun is setting. What a day. Bryce is carrying Kendall with one arm and has my hand with his free one. I look up and notice the smile on his face. Anyone passing by would think he is a happy groom who just attached himself to the woman of his dreams.

"So why don't you let us take Kendall for the night? You guys can go out to a nice dinner, spend a little down time before getting back to the real world tomorrow," Karen suggests.

"What do you say, Darryn?" Bryce looks down at me, giving me a slight nod saying he thinks it sounds like a good idea.

"I don't know, I have never been away from her overnight, plus I didn't bring anything extra for her."

"Don't be upset, Darryn, but today Kendall and I did a little shopping." Karen holds her arms out and Kendall goes right to her.

"Trust me when I say, she won't be needing extra clothes when she is at our house," Steven adds, rolling his eyes.

"All right, all right. I went a little crazy, but we had fun, didn't we?" Karen tickles Kendall's tummy and she giggles, then wraps her arms around Karen's neck in a tight hug.

"Do you want to stay with Grandma Karen tonight?" I ask her.

Karen's head swings toward me, tears shining in her eyes. "I hope you don't mind?" I ask.

The smile on her face answers for her. "No, of course not, I'm honored you even suggested it. So does this mean we can have a sleepover tonight?"

I look up at Bryce, he nods his head. "It will be all right."

"All right, we can try it," I agree, but my stomach is in knots. Today has been a whirlwind of changes.

CHAPTER EIGHTEEN

Bryce

"So do you have any preferences on what you would like for dinner?" I ask, needing to break the silence in the car.

I know her head must be spinning. If I am being honest with myself, mine is a little as well. We just got married. Strange how all day I was fine, sure a little nervous, but that was expected. Right now, driving in silence, it all seems to settle in. Darryn just sits there, looking out the passenger window, her elbow on the door's arm rest, her chin resting in her hand. My nerves probably aren't from realizing I'm a married man now, but more from wondering what is going through her mind.

Her shoulders shrug and she takes a deep breath. She doesn't face me, but she does turn her head to look out the front windshield. "I know your mom took Kendall so we can have a nice dinner and all, but really, Bryce, I'm not expecting anything special. We can just grab something fast on the way to your house."

I want to pull over and shake her. I'm pretty sure that wouldn't do any good. She looks defeated and that is bothering me. I know this isn't the ideal way for her to handle things, marrying a man she didn't know that well in order to be protected from her psychotic ex. There is a small part of me hoping that when this is all over, she will want to stay with me, but watching her right now is not giving me much hope of her wanting to stay. Just the thought of her leaving feels like someone punched me in the chest. I need to use this time to convince her that my feelings are more than just to protect her and Kendall. They both have my heart fully. Now I just need to figure out a way to make her see that.

I know the perfect place to eat. It is one of my favorite restaurants along the boardwalk. Turning into the parking lot, I notice the puzzled look on Darryn's face. "Look, we haven't had a real date, just the two of us yet. What more of a perfect time than our wedding day?"

Darryn just sits there for a moment looking out the front window. Her laughter shocks me when it bubbles out of her. Her head resting against the headrest of her seat, she turns and looks at me for the first time since we got into the car with a smile on her lips. "You can always make me smile, thank you."

"Well what are husbands for?" I grab her hand and kiss it. "Would you please honor me by joining me for dinner tonight, Darryn?"

"How is a girl supposed to say no to that?"

"I'm hoping that you can't say no."

"It seems that I have a very hard time telling you no, my husband."

It shocks me to hear her call me her husband, but I think it surprises her more to say it by the look in her eyes. She almost seems embarrassed. She tries pulling her hand away from mine, but I don't let go, I need her to stop wanting to pull away from me physically and mentally. I know the word was used to prove her point of saying yes when I asked her to marry me, but just hearing it out of her mouth catches us both by surprise I think. Personally, I like the way it sounds coming from her.

"Would my wife please join me for dinner tonight?" I ask again, hoping to help her feel a little more comfortable with her earlier choice of wording.

"I would love to." She squeezes my hand and it takes everything in me not to pull her over onto my lap and kiss her.

Dinner has gone well but when Darryn asks me for the tenth time to check my phone to make sure my mom hasn't called, or looks at hers for the hundredth time, I am ready to throw them both on the tray of the next passing server.

"Darryn, I know this must be stressful for you, the first time away from Kendall, but trust me, she is in good hands. My mom has the largest collection of Disney movies you have ever seen. They are probably having a movie marathon, complete with popcorn and candy," I try to reassure her.

Darryn puts her phone down on the table, face up, so that she can't have any chance of missing a call from my mom. "I'm sorry."

"Don't apologize, just try and relax a little. By the way, when you called my mom Grandma Karen to Kendall today, you made her day." I remember the way my mom's eyes beamed when she heard her new title to Kendall. All she has talked about the last few years is when either of us were planning on settling down and giving her grandbabies to spoil. Now that she has one, there will be no holding back for her.

"Like you said earlier, a child can't have too many grandparents in their life. Kendall has none, so if she were to ever have one, I would want them to be as sweet as your mother."

"I'm going to warn you, there is going to be a lot of spoiling, just prepare and before you can argue about it, there is nothing any of us can do to stop it, so just let it happen. Trust me, we would be in a lot more trouble with the spoiling if Charliee knew about all of this, she loves children."

Darryn's smile drops and she looks down at her plate. "I'm sorry."

"For what?"

"I know this can't be easy to keep from your brother and sister." She is playing with her napkin and again, she won't look at me.

"I didn't tell Derrick about us getting married, but I did tell him you were moving into my place. He has a tendency to stop by a lot, so I figured I'd let him know you will be there. We have both agreed it would be better to keep Charliee out of everything. She is still home recovering and she needs to concentrate on that, not worry about all of us right now."

"Another thing I'm sorry about. Your family should only be concentrating on Charliee, not having to be pulled into my problems."

Reaching across the table, I take her hands in mine. "Darryn, stop, all right! We are all taking care of Charliee. I don't want to spend this evening with you worrying all night and me trying to convince you everything is going to work out. It's a nice night, why don't we go for a walk on the beach before we head home. Trust me, starting tomorrow there will be plenty of time to worry about everything and work out all the details; for tonight, let's just relax and enjoy the evening."

When she looks up at me, I see that she wants to argue with me and I'm ready for it, but instead she surprises me by taking a deep breath and just nods her head.

"Does that mean you are good with the walk on the beach?" I ask, hoping so because I have something in mind.

"Yes, that sounds nice."

I get the attention of our waiter and pay the bill. I take her hand as we leave the restaurant and lead her down to the water. There is still a chill in the air, which is nice because that means there aren't a lot of people down here. We walk a little distance and when no one is around that I can see, I stop and pull my phone out of my pocket.

"Is everything all right? Is your mom calling?" Darryn tries looking over at my phone's screen.

"Darryn, breathe, no one is calling me." I flip through my phone to find my music, and finding the song I want, I hit play.

"Every bride should be able to have a first dance on her wedding day." I hold my hand out to her as the song begins to play.

She doesn't move, she just stares down at my hand. "Come on, Darryn, dance with me."

Looking up at me, there is enough light from the moon that I can see the shine in her eyes from her tears. No longer waiting, I take her hand in mine, wrap my arm around her waist and pull her into me. She doesn't resist, but it does take a moment for her to move. Finally, her arms wrap up around my shoulders. I wrap my other arm around her waist, pulling her tight against me, and she surprises me when she rests her head against my chest. At that moment, I know I'm not going to be able to let her go when all of this was over.

CHAPTER NINETEEN

Darryn

What have I done to deserve a guy like this in my life? Actually, this is more like a cruel joke being played on me. I'm being given this amazing guy only to have him be pulled away from me later. As soon as this is all over with Brett, Bryce will want a divorce and I will have to let him go. He pulls me closer into him when he wraps his other arm around my waist and I just want to melt into his chest. It's a little unnerving on how safe I feel when I'm in his arms. I don't feel the need to look over my shoulder, I don't have the feeling like someone is watching me. I don't really have any cares to be honest. Right now, all I want to do is get closer to Bryce.

"Are you all right?" Bryce's voice breaks through my daze.

I nod against his chest. "Yeah, I'm good. This is sweet of you."

Bryce pulls back to look down at me. The heat cools in my cheek instantly without his body against my face. "Well, your wedding day should be something you always remember."

I laugh, always remember! How could someone forget a day like today? "Bryce, I can promise you I will never forget today. I woke up this morning and agreed to marry a man I've only really known for a couple weeks. Someone I have only had one date with, someone who is protecting me against my crazed ex. Trust me, I will never forget today."

He reads me like a book, however I can never guess what is going through his mind. Like right now, he is staring at me like he really wants to say something, but what I have no clue. I can see he is debating with himself.

"Bryce, what is it, what's going through that mind of yours?"

I watch as his eyes change to that crystal color again. I know what that means, my whole body heats up in anticipation. There is a look of questioning in his eyes; he isn't going to make the first move, he doesn't want to push me. He is afraid of how I may react, too much too fast.

Pushing up onto my toes, I bring his head down to mine, our lips lightly brush against each other's. Bryce takes a deep breath.

"Please kiss me, Bryce." It comes out sounding like I am begging, but right now I don't care. I will be more than happy to beg this man to kiss me.

"Darryn, don't do anything you don't want to, I'm not expecting anything from you."

"Bryce, kiss me!" This time I demand it, bringing his lips

back down to mine, not giving him the chance to try and talk me out of it.

I'm surprised when he groans and pulls me up tight against his chest again. Almost like he is afraid I will change my mind and pull away from him. How wrong he is. All I can think about is a way to get closer. The kiss is deep, when his tongue finds mine I hear myself moan. I want more of him, I want all of him, not just his lips. Sliding my hands under his shirt, my knees buckle when I feel his skin, warm and toned under my hands. Something snaps inside of me, I need this man and I want him now.

Pushing his shirt up, I'm shocked when he quickly pulls away from me and out of my reach. Instantly I realize what I was about to do. My cheeks instantly burn and I can't look up at him. What the hell is wrong with me? Here is a guy who is trying to protect me in any way that he can and here I am trying to strip him on a public beach. Grabbing my hand, he leads me off the beach and back toward the restaurant. I hadn't even noticed the group of teenagers until we passed them walking back. Now I'm mortified. Not only did I throw myself at him, but I caused a scene in public while doing it. No wonder he is pissed at me.

He hasn't said a word, he basically drags me along as he quickly makes our way back to his car. He opens my door, shutting it as I sit down in the passenger seat. I want to crawl in the back seat and hide, or jump out and run as far away from Bryce as I can get. Folding my hands into my lap, I curl myself into the door, looking only out the window, wishing I had the strength to just jump from the car.

Not a word is said all the way back to Bryce's house. Can I blame him? When we pull up to the house, I quickly get out of the car and run up to the front door. All I want to do is go to my room and hide. Turning the door knob, I swear under my breath. Damn it, it's locked. All I can do now is wait for Bryce.

Before I know it, he is by my side, quickly unlocking the door. He opens it and I push myself past him only to be stopped by him. Grabbing my arm, he stops me at the same time he slams the front door shut. Before I know what's happening, my back is against the door. Bryce's arms have me trapped, one on each side of my head, his body tightly against mine. His breathing is heavy; I can't look at him though.

"Look at me, Darryn."

All I can do is shake my head no. I can't look at him. I just want to go to my room and hide until Brett can be found and I can leave.

"Damn it, Darryn, look at me please."

My eyes fly up to his. This is a tone I haven't heard from Bryce. When our eyes meet, I'm surprised to find his eyes are crystal again. "I'm so sorry, Bryce, I don't know what came over me."

"I'm not sorry, Darryn, and I don't want you to be sorry. I want you, I'm not hiding that from you, but I'm not going to do that in a public place and in front of a bunch of teenagers. Tell me no, and I will let you go to bed right now. Tell me yes, and I'm taking you to my bed tonight, and I can't make you any promises that if I have you tonight, that I'll be able to not have you in my bed every night."

I don't know what to say. He isn't pissed at me. I can see that now in his eyes. He is giving me a choice, but along with that choice is a promise. Every night in Bryce's bed sounds very tempting, but it will make it all that much harder when I have to say goodbye. His lips are only inches away from mine. I can feel his chest rub against mine with every breath he takes. My brain is telling me to run and fast. My body is begging me to have this man. I'm so tired of always being cautious. Always doing the right thing hoping to fix all the mistakes I have made in the past. I don't want to think anymore; I want to live.

Looking up into his pleading eyes, I bring my hands up and under his shirt. His breath hitches the moment my hands touch his skin. Running my hands up his sides, over his chest, I bring the shirt up as I go. He pushes away from me and removes his shirt, letting it fall to the floor. Before I have a chance to enjoy the vision in front of me, one of Bryce's arms links around my waist pulling me tightly against him, his lips claiming mine with a hunger that's hard to deny, along with his hardness pressing into my pelvis. My center heats up instantly, begging for what he is offering. Before I know what's happening, he hooks an arm under my knees, picking me up without breaking our kiss. I know where we are headed and I find myself becoming nervous.

Feeling the softness of Bryce's bed sends a shock through me, so much so that I break our kiss.

"Are you all right? You can stop me, Darryn, I'm not going to force you into anything." Concern is etched in his eyes.

I know he will never force me, I have never feared Bryce. Can I do this and not fall for him more than I already have? I already know it's going to tear me apart when we have to part ways, if I add a physical relationship into the deal it may destroy me. Looking up into his eyes, I find myself melting. There is a need and want in those eyes. He wants me, maybe he won't want to end this. Just maybe we can make it work. I'm always having to look into the future. Worrying and having a plan for if Brett finds us. I can't live in the moment or let my guard down. Right now, I want to live in the moment.

Not worry about what will happen tomorrow, just enjoy the now.

"I don't want you to stop, Bryce," I tell him before I can change my mind again and become the sensible person I usually have to be.

Please don't ask me again if I'm sure, I think to myself. I don't want to think any longer, the more I think about it the better the possibility I will chicken out and go to my own room tonight.

Bryce stares at me for a moment, I'm afraid he may be the one to pull away now. I hope my eyes aren't telling him how scared I am, but how much I want and need him as well. Hooking my hand around the back of his neck, I pull his lips back down to mine. He doesn't pull away, his lips start out tender. Running my fingers up into his hair, I deepen the kiss and am rewarded with a deep moan from him. At that point my mind clears from all doubt and my body takes over.

Bryce works us up so that I am now sitting in front of him, but never breaks our kiss. I feel his knuckles skim across my ribs as he pulls my shirt up and over my head, letting it drop to the floor, my bra quickly following. My hands travel down to the waist of his pants. Unbuttoning them, I can feel his hardness begging to be released from the tight denim. I slip my hands into the backside, under his boxer briefs, and push them all down over his legs.

Bryce steps out of his pants and before I can sit here for too long and enjoy the breathtaking man in front of me, he gently pushes me back against the bed. My hands on his chest, I move them down, exploring the many muscles running along his chest and stomach. Bryce's lips start on my neck, placing small kisses as he moves down my throat to the top mound of one of my breasts. I can feel my nipple tighten with want. He trails small kisses from one breast, to the valley in between my breasts to the top of the other, and then all around the nipple, taking care not to touch the nipple begging to be touched. I dig my nails into his backside and arch my back, hoping he will end the torturous teasing. I can feel the moisture and heat from my center and I am yet to feel his naked body against mine. It's all part of his slow tease he is torturing me with right now. I want to beg him, but part of me wants him to continue. It's a very confusing feeling, one that only drives the need that much more.

His lips move down over my ribs and down my stomach to the waist of my pants. It takes everything in me not to push him away and strip the rest of my own clothes off and then push him back down onto the bed. His tongue lightly skims over my skin from one hip bone to the other, my hips thrust up on their own, begging. When he pulls back, I almost scream out, no!

His eyes never leave mine as his hands go to work on unbuttoning my jeans. I know he is watching for any signs that I am changing my mind and want him to stop. He is still worried that I may not be ready or wanting this. No words I can say will convince him that I'm completely ready and having no doubts, so instead I'm going to have to show him.

Sitting up, I push him back a little and stand in front of him. I finish removing the rest of my clothes, stepping out of them, my eyes never leaving his. We both stand here for a moment, not a word spoken, eyes locked with each other. I need his touch; it's not a want, it's very much a need at this point. I'm going to drop to my knees and beg for his touch in second. Not being able to stand it any longer, I close the space between us and hear both of us moan the moment our bodies touch. Fire shoots through every vein in my body and slams into my core all at once. My lips find his in a hunger I have never experienced before. I want to climb up his body and wrap my legs around his hips. I can feel his hardness pressing against my stomach, my core is begging for it. I'm ready, I can feel how hot and wet I am.

I swear I hear a deep growl come from Bryce, but before I have any time to think about it, I'm picked up and we are both now on the bed, myself laying under Bryce. Something has changed, he is no longer holding back or being cautious. His hungry mouth finally takes one very hard nipple and he sucks hard. I almost lose myself right then. My core pulses with need. I arch my back and with my hands at the back of his head, press his head down, begging him to suck harder. His mouth moves from one breast to the other, I hold back the scream that threatens to escape.

Lost in a daze of need, I don't realize he has moved his way down my body until I feel his hot breath against my hot center. I shoot up off the bed, my eyes flying wide open. He just smiles up at me and his eyes never leave mine as I watch his tongue dart out to taste my very wet center. He moans, and I try to hold it together. My head falls back, my arms are shaking trying to hold me up. Bryce spreads my legs so that he can taste me deeper and I can't hold it in any longer, I fall back against the bed, my hands clutching the bed sheets and my body shaking uncontrollably with release. Before my head clears enough to think, I feel Bryce quickly bring himself back up, his lips take mine and he quickly enters me. I scream against his lips. I'm so tight and he is now filling me completely, I can already feel another release. How is that even possible? He pulls out and thrusts back in, I can feel myself convulse around him, pulling him deeper and deeper inside with each thrust. I wrap my legs around his waist, needing him even deeper. He quickens the pace and I'm not sure how I'm going to make it through this release that is building, I try to hold it back, but I think that just might make it more intense.

"Come on, Darryn, let go, I can't hold back much longer," his husky voice begs me and that is my undoing. My body explodes around him. I feel Bryce's body tense and his mouth crushes against mine as we share our release.

Bryce is still kissing me gently as my body relaxes from what I would say is the most intense sexual experience I have ever had. I didn't know sex could feel like that.

"Are you all right?" Bryce whispers in my ear.

I shiver from the feel of his warm breath in my ear. I feel that stirring in my core again. There is no way I can make it through another experience like the last one again tonight. My body obviously is thinking differently. Bryce is still inside of me, and every time he kisses the side of my neck and then up to my ear, his body moves against mine, and inside of me. I'm exhausted, but my body is very awake and alert. My hips begin to move with his, Bryce groans against my neck and it vibrates through my entire body.

"What are you doing to me, Darryn?"

What am I doing to him? I think I should be the one asking that question to him.

CHAPTER TWENTY

Bryce

I feel Darryn's body starting to move with mine. I didn't intend to go for another round, but I am still hard inside of her. Even after a release like I just experienced with this amazing woman, I'm ready for another. I can't seem to get enough of her.

Earlier I told her if she came to bed with me tonight, I wouldn't be able to let her sleep in the other room afterwards. I knew if she said that was where she was staying, I would have put the white flag up and slept alone, but now after having her, I'm pretty sure I am going to do whatever is needed to make sure I have her in my bed every night. This just sealed the deal with me. I know I'm going to do what needs to be done to try and keep her from wanting to leave after we ended this thing with her ex. I'm in love with this woman, hands down, no questions asked, there are no doubts in my mind. Now you add the chemistry between us in the bedroom and it's a sealed deal as far as I'm concerned.

We both need to be up early in the morning for work. It's been an emotional and very busy couple of days, I know she needs her rest. I should let her get some sleep, but now with her body starting to sway with mine again, sleep is going to have to wait just a little longer. If it means being exhausted tomorrow at work because I spent the evening inside of this woman, then it will be completely worth it.

That's when I realize it, one of the reasons why I'm pretty sure this feels so much different and better, I used no protection! The realization feels like cold water being dumped on my entire body. What the hell has gotten into me?

"Bryce, what's wrong?" Darryn's voice sounds concerned.

How can I have been so negligent? I know how, it is this woman in my arms. I can't think of anything else other than being inside of her.

"Darryn, I forgot protection." I have never slept with a woman without protection, even if she told me she was covered.

Silence stretched throughout the room. I'm ready for her to push me away, but she hasn't moved.

"Darryn, I'm so sorry. That's not like me at all. I promise you I have never had unprotected sex, and I have a physical with work yearly. I'm clean."

Still nothing from her. I start to pull away from her, the silence from her I assume means she is completely pissed off and I can't blame her for being mad at me. She surprises me when her hands slide down to my backside, stopping me from pulling out of her.

"Bryce, don't put all the blame on yourself. I should have

asked. I'm on the pill so we are covered in that sense. I just had my physical with work and everything came back clean."

I can't see her face in the dark room, but she doesn't sound mad. If I had any doubts, they are quickly dismissed when she pushes me over onto my back, now with her straddled on top of me, which pushes me even deeper inside of her. Sitting myself up, her legs wrap around my waist and her arms go around my shoulders. My hands travel down to her hips and I claim her lips. Sliding her body back just enough to where only the tip of my hardness is still inside her, I thrust deep back into her. Her legs tighten around my waist, her nails digging into my shoulder blades. It doesn't take long before we are both tightly holding onto the other in a release so intense, I swear I might have blacked out for a moment.

Sitting here for a moment, neither of us move. We just stay wrapped tightly around the other. Her body begins to relax against mine and her arms loosen around my neck, but her body stays pressed against mine, her head resting on my shoulder. After a moment, I can hear her even, soft breathing. Smiling, I realize she has fallen asleep. Carefully, I pull her arms from around my shoulders and maneuver us apart, not a very easy task from this position. Stretching out on the bed, I pull her down with me and instantly she snuggles up against my side, and tugs at my heart with the little sigh of content-ment that releases from her lips. I have never had a woman sleep with me in my bed, but with Darryn it feels right. This is where she belongs, now all I have to do is convince her to stay.

"Man, you look exhausted, but oddly very content, if that makes any sense." Derrick smirks over at me from the driver's side of our patrol car.

He is searching for information. It is killing him not knowing everything about the situation between Darryn and myself. If I'm being honest, it is killing me not being able to tell him everything. I want to tell him how amazing she is and her daughter, but that would start too many questions and I made a promise to Darryn.

I am exhausted, even though I think last night was the best sleep I have ever had. Sleeping next to Darryn was comforting. When the alarm went off this morning, she jumped out of bed, which made me jump out of bed. She ran into the room that she and Kendall have been sharing without even a word. I wanted to go after her and make her talk to me, but I decided to give her a little time instead. When I walked past the bedroom door to head to the kitchen for some coffee, I heard her talking in the room. I assumed she called my mom to check on Kendall. When she finally came out to the kitchen, she was dressed and ready for work. Our conversation this morning before we left the house consisted of her meeting me at the station after work, leaving her car there, and the two of us heading to my parents' house to pick up Kendall. She wouldn't even look me in the eyes, she just moved around the kitchen, pretending to be busy as we talked so that she wouldn't have to look at me. She did text me when she got to work this morning like I asked her to before she left.

"It's been crazy the last couple of days trying to help Darryn with this ex-boyfriend situation."

"Are you sure you haven't gotten too invested in this situation?" Derrick gives me that smirk, he isn't talking about the ex-boyfriend. He is fishing for information about the living situation between Darryn and myself.

"Why is it so hard for you to believe that I'm just trying to help her? Why does it have to be a sexual thing with you?

Maybe that's you, but not me," I say, feeling a little guilty because after last night, it became a personal thing as well.

"Because, I was there every time you asked her out, and you just don't move a woman and her daughter into your house to protect them. You could have gone through the department and put them in a safe house or something. Instead, you have decided to play the hero and take care of all of it yourself. The only reason there is a report is because she ended up at the station the other night because she thought she was being followed. So, do you want to tell me what is really going on here?"

I need to give him something, he knows me too well and obviously I'm not fooling him. I should have known it wouldn't be that easy. If the situation was turned then I wouldn't believe him either.

"Honestly, our main focus right now is her ex. I'm not going to say I'm not still interested in her, but if you think I only moved her in for that reason you are wrong. I do care about her and her daughter, trust me, once you meet that little one you are a goner. After her telling me everything he has done to her, I just want to make sure nothing happens to either one of them. Everything kind of happened fast, but I don't regret any decisions that have been made."

Hopefully this is enough info for him to lay off the subject for a little while. I admitted to it being a little more than just a protection detail, that's what he wants to hear. He just wants me to admit that I like Darryn.

Derrick sits there staring at me, like he is trying to look into my head and see if there is more or something. "Well, at least you are admitting to it being a little more than just being the cop protecting the girl." He laughs at me.

"I see that you have Mom watching her little one?" Derrick asks next.

How did he know it was Kendall? I almost ask, but then remember the night Darryn's apartment was broken into, Derrick was there. "When did you go over there?"

"Last night after work, I stopped by for a minute. I walked in and she came running out of the living room when she heard my voice, but she was calling me Bryce. It took me a minute to figure out who she was at first, the day of the break in at their apartment had a lot going on, and then I remembered you telling me Mom was going to be watching her. She almost ran right into me but stopped right before she wrapped her arms around my legs and just stared up at me, like she knew I wasn't you."

"Smart girl."

My heart skips a little. Kendall may have been confused but she knew something was different, she sensed that Derrick wasn't me. There are adults who have known us our entire lives that can't figure out who is who.

"Ha-ha! Do you think having her with Mom and Dad is safe? I mean if there is someone following Darryn, and she goes to their house to pick up her daughter, what's to stop them from going back there later? Don't get me wrong, she needs to be in a safe place, and Mom will do anything to keep that little one safe, but isn't that kind of bringing trouble to Mom and Dad?"

I know what Derrick is trying to say. It is something I thought about a lot actually. This is my choice to be involved as much as I am, and I'm possibly bringing danger to our parents.

"I have hopefully created a solution to that problem. Either I will go and pick up Kendall and drop her off, or if

Darryn does go she isn't in her car, she is with me. Trust me, this whole situation has been very thoroughly thought out, I hope. It's complicated, I'll admit to that, and hopefully it's all over fast and we find this guy and put him away before anything gets to that."

"Bryce, I'm not trying to say you haven't thought of everything, I'm sure you have a pretty good plan in order, but something is always missed, or someone slips up. I don't want to sound like an ass and say Mom and Dad are more important than this little girl, but..."

I stop him, I know what he means. "Derrick, trust me, this is the last thing I wanted. I was talking to Mom and she offered."

"Come on, Bryce, you know if you tell Mom anyone is in trouble, especially if you are adding a child into the equation, she is going to jump in and offer to help. We have been through so much with this whole situation with Charliee and almost losing her, now we are going to add this to everything."

Derrick is getting mad. I really can't blame him. "Derrick, I have Darryn meeting me at the station and parking her car in the back behind the gates at night after work and then she leaves with me, we then go and pick up Kendall. My windows are tinted, you can't even see the passenger in my car. He has no idea who I am or if we have any kind of connection. Mom and Dad are going to be fine."

"Famous last words!"

The call over radio cuts our conversation short. Probably a good thing, any longer and I would have had to take the side of my new family against my brother, who has no idea I have a family now, and piss him off thinking I'm endangering my own family for a girl and her child. If he knew this guy was after his sister-in-law and niece, this conversation would be going in a completely different direction. Not that my brother doesn't care. He does and I know that, I understand what he is saying, it has run through my head a million times and I have done everything I can think of to make sure my parents never have any trouble.

We pull out onto the street, sirens blaring, on our way to a traffic accident. The drive there is in complete silence. Just before we reach the scene, I can't take it any longer.

"Derrick, I need your help finding this asshole."

"I may not agree with everything you have chosen to do, and I'll be honest with you, Bryce, I feel like you are keeping something from me and it bugs the hell out of me, but I would never not have your back. If you need me I'm here, you should never question that."

Before I can say anything back, we approach the accident and have to get to work. I've never questioned if my brother would help if I asked for it, but I have to admit it is nice to hear him say it.

CHAPTER TWENTY-ONE

Darryn

"All right, Tom, I can't take the silent treatment any longer. Talk to me."

All day, Tom has only answered the questions asked to him. I have gotten the silent treatment other than that.

"What would you like me to say, Darryn?"

"Right now I really don't care. Yell at me if it makes you feel better, just don't keep giving me the silent treatment, I can't take it."

I had called Tom and told him about Brett and everything that has happened, up to when he was following me the other day. Bryce asked me to. He wanted to make sure I was watched when he wasn't around.

"What do you want me to say?" he asks, his tone flat.

"Anything right now would work. I know you are upset, I'm just not sure about what part."

We have been driving around all day. Usually between calls, we stop, chat for a while and wait for the next call to come in. Today has been slow, which I'm not saying is a bad thing, but it has made for a lot of silent time and driving, basically in circles.

Finally, Tom pulls into a parking lot and throws the rig into park, then turns to me. "Not sure about what part? How about all of it, Darryn?"

"All of it?" I ask back.

"Hell yes, all of it. You are hiding from someone and I get that it's hard to trust people, but I would have thought by now you would have trusted us instead of thinking you needed to take this all on alone. Yet you go on a date one time with a guy and he knows everything, and before me might I add."

That's what this is all about? Tom is mad because Bryce knew about all of this before he did?

"Tom, he is a cop, he was there when my place got broken into."

I'm not about to tell him I called Bryce when I first found out someone had been in my place, that he wasn't even on duty that day. Tom may throw me out of the vehicle if I tell him that part.

"Darryn, it's not just that, you are staying with a guy you barely know. Don't get me wrong, Bryce is a great guy, I've known him and his brother for a while now. I know you are safe there with him and knowing him like I do, he will take care of you and Kendall..."

"Wait, Tom, are you mad because I didn't call and ask to stay with you guys?" I interrupt him when I figure out what this is all about finally.

"Darryn, you aren't getting it. It's not just one thing, it's the whole thing. We have been partners now for a while, I thought we had a friendship where you trusted us, that's all."

"Tom, you and Heather are the first friends I have had in years. All my partners before you I barely talked to while we were working, let alone went to their house for dinner. I lost all my friends throughout the time I was with Brett. By the time I finally found enough nerve to leave him, I had no friends left, and I had no family even before him. My situation isn't something I brag to people about. Trust me, there were a couple times I thought about talking to you, you are very easy to open up to, but I didn't want you looking at me differently."

"What do you mean by that?"

"I didn't want you to know the weak side of me. I'm not proud of that time in my life. Allowing myself to be in that kind of relationship. To be honest, if I wouldn't have gotten pregnant with Kendall I may never have left, so basically she saved my life."

Tom starts to say something, but I stop him. I don't need him to sit here and tell me that I'm not weak, I left, that makes me a strong person and all of that. Like Bryce, Tom would never understand because he has never had to live it.

"Tom, you have a home, with a beautiful family. I didn't want to bring all of this to you guys. I could never do anything that I thought might endanger your family because of my mistakes and this mistake may very well follow me home one day, literally!"

Tom just sits there staring at me for a moment. I study him as he thinks about everything I have just told him, that's when I see the look I dread, he feels sorry for me.

"Please, Tom, don't look at me that way."

"What way is that?"

"Sorry for me."

"It's not what you are thinking, Darryn. You think I'm feeling sorry for you because of what you went through and for having no one in your life to turn to. That's not it at all. I feel sorry for you because you don't see what an amazing person you are. How strong you are. It may have taken you getting pregnant to leave, but you did it, regardless of the circumstances that led up to it. You had no one to help you once you did leave. You found a safe spot for your baby and yourself, and you found a way to support the both of you starting with nothing. You have made a home for yourself and Kendall. She is happy and healthy. That's not the actions of a weak person, Darryn. You have far more strength than a lot of people, you just refuse to see it."

I feel a tear roll down my cheek and I quickly wipe it away. These last couple of days have been an emotional roller coaster and it is exhausting, but for the first time in a very long time something feels different. My chest used to feel heavy, like a ton of bricks were just sitting there. One by one these last couple of days it feels like those bricks are being taken off, my chest feels lighter. I know this is all far from over, it won't be over until Brett can no longer hurt either one of us, but I don't have to do it alone anymore.

"You need to realize what an amazing person you are, Darryn, and if it's the last thing I do, you will start to see it."

"Thank you, Tom, for everything you and Heather have done for us. I am so sorry."

"Bryce just better not be making you sleep on the couch."

My smile fades, sleeping on the couch, no. *He should be making me sleep in my own bed though*, I think to myself, thinking back to last night. Last night was amazing. I have never experienced anything like I did last night with Bryce.

"Why are your cheeks turning red, Darryn? What is going on over there between the two of you?"

I quickly turn my face away from Tom and look out the side window. Now if that doesn't look guilty, I don't know how more obvious I could be.

"Bryce has given us his spare bedroom to use."

"Are you using the spare bedroom?" Tom asks accusingly.

"Yes, sleeping with a two-year-old is a ton of fun, so if I come to work grumpy you now know why." I look back at him, hoping that with a little eye contact it will convince him everything is only a friend's relationship status with Bryce and I and we can change the direction of this conversation.

He isn't buying it, it is written all over that smug smile he is giving me. "It's all right to like him, Darryn."

Like him, I'm married to him! I want to yell out. The ring hanging against my chest feels like it is burning me.

"Sorry, I didn't mean to tease you. However, it is all right to like the guy. You are allowed to be happy, Darryn. Our shift is almost over, so before we head back, just one last thing and I will let it drop. No more secrets, from this point on you let me know what's going on. Promise?"

I just nod my head. There already is another secret, one that when he does find out, I'm sure there will be no end to his wrath when that all comes out in the open.

"All right, well let's get back, and then I'm going to follow you to the station."

Follow me to the station, when did that happen? I never asked him to do that.

"Bryce called me this morning," he answers my question before I can ask it. "Don't even try and argue with me about it, I will be following you each day after work to the station."

I just take a deep breath and sit back in my seat. I know

they all think they are doing their best to help me, but in the midst of helping me they are all putting their families in danger and I'm not feeling real good about that.

When I arrive at the station, Bryce is waiting for me. My face instantly heats up the second he looks at me and smiles. We haven't talked about last night. This morning when his alarm went off, I jumped out of the bed and basically ran to the spare room. I was waiting for him to come knock on the door, or catch me in the hallway coming out of the bathroom and insist that we talk, but he didn't. I got ready and sat in the room for a little while trying to dodge the whole thing, but realized I would have to eventually leave to go to work, and I really wanted some coffee before we left. Taking a deep breath, I entered the kitchen, but to my surprise he never brought it up. He was all calm and cool leaning up against the counter, drinking coffee and looking at his phone. He said good morning and then asked if I was ready to go. I was relieved and disappointed all at the same time. What had I expected? I jumped out of bed and ran out like the room was on fire.

Walking up to him, he looks over my shoulder and stretches out his hand. Crap, I forgot Tom followed me into the station. I told him I was fine, but he insisted.

"Thanks, Tom," Bryce said as he shook his hand.

"No problem. I will meet you guys here tomorrow morning and make sure she gets to work," Tom offers.

"That's not necessary..." I start but am cut off by Bryce.

"I appreciate that, but we have a car that is going to follow a little ways back, we are hoping to catch him following her at some point," Bryce explains.

I, on the other hand, am starting to get a little pissed. They are both talking like I'm not even standing in front of them.

"Hello," I say to Bryce, who hasn't said a word to me yet. Why that bothered me so much, I'm not sure.

Tom laughs behind me. "Let me know if you need anything. See you tomorrow, Darryn." Then he walks away.

Bryce looks down at me with an amused look on his face. "Were you feeling a little left out?" he asks.

"You guys were talking like I wasn't even standing here. When were you going to tell me you were going to have me followed?"

"Darryn, you haven't said more than a couple of words to me since last night. You shot out of bed so fast this morning, you seemed like you couldn't get away from me fast enough."

I look around to see who is close enough to be able to hear our conversation. No one is around, I take a deep breath. I don't think the whole station needs to know what is going on between the two of us, where Bryce, on the other hand, doesn't seem to care who may be around to hear our conversation.

"Can we please go now? I would rather not talk about this here, plus I've missed Kendall and I'm ready to go pick her up now."

Bryce points down the hall toward the back of the station. "Lead the way."

The drive over to Bryce's parents' house is quiet. Bryce asks how my day was, if I had talked more to Tom, but nothing about last night. He isn't going to bring it up, he is waiting for me to say something. Once we walk into the front door to pick up Kendall, she comes running down the hall and into Bryce's arms. My heart stops for a moment. I have always been her world, the one she ran to, now everything is about Bryce and I'm not quite sure how I feel about that. I'm happy she likes Bryce, it definitely makes our living arrangement easier, but I'm not used to sharing her attention.

Once home, Bryce goes out and throws a few hamburgers on the grill, I give Kendall a bath, and we eat dinner. Bryce and Kendall are in full conversation of her overnight stay with Grandma Karen and Grandpa Steve. It does warm my heart to hear her talking about how much fun she had. How Karen and Steve have accepted her with open arms. Bedtime story doesn't last long for her. I don't think I make it off page three before she is sound asleep. I just keep reading the story out loud.

Kendall has her bed here now, I am going to just use the bed Bryce already had in here. My bed went into storage. I should go out and talk to Bryce, I just don't know what to say. We have nothing else to talk about except the events of last night, and I'm not sure what we need to talk about. I look over at the bed I will be using and it looks empty, lonely. Last night was one of the best night's sleep I have had in a very long time. Being with Bryce last night was amazing all around. I have never experienced feelings like I had last night, but the best part wasn't the sex, which was amazing, it was the sleeping. I felt safe. I didn't feel like I had to be on alert. I hate to admit it but I don't want to sleep alone tonight, I want to be in Bryce's arms again.

I can't sit here all night. It is still pretty early. I can hear the television on in the front room. If I sit here all night Bryce will know I'm avoiding him, I just don't want him thinking it's for the reason he will believe it's for. I'm pretty sure he is thinking I regret last night. I want to slap myself, what the hell is wrong with me? How old am I? I'm an adult and I need to start acting like one. We need to talk about this, we can't live under the same roof and act like last night didn't happen.

Tucking Kendall in, I figure it's time to go out and face Bryce. Taking a deep breath, I walk out of our room and down the hall. I find Bryce sitting on the couch, a beer in hand, his socked feet propped up on the coffee table, watching television.

"I brought you a beer as well, but it may be a little warm now." He points at a beer sitting on the table.

I understand his meaning. I have been in the room for a while, but I didn't realize how long until I look at the clock hanging on the wall, it is almost ten.

"Yeah! Um, sorry about that, I fell asleep for a moment as well," I lied. When I look over at him, I can see he knows I'm lying.

I want to run back to the room, why is this so hard to talk to him about? I watch as Bryce picks up the remote control and turns off the show he is watching.

He pats the couch cushion next to him. "Darryn, we need to talk."

Nodding, I walk over and sit down, but not next to him on the couch. I take the chair.

"Darryn, I've tried to wait for you to talk to me, but that isn't working, so I'm going to bring up last night. We need to talk about it."

Again, I just nod. How does one even start a conversation of this kind of subject?

"Do you regret it?" he asks point blank.

I guess that's how you start this kind of conversation, just go straight to the point. Now how to answer the question. I can tell him yes, I regret it and then he will probably tell me that he is sorry and swear it will never happen again, and knowing Bryce, it won't happen again. And that's what I fear if I'm being honest with myself. I think my fear is that I'm already starting to have feelings for him, and repeats of last night are only going to grow those feelings, and then how do I leave him when that time comes without destroying my heart?

Bryce stands up from the couch and crouches down in front of me. "Darryn, please talk to me."

I can't lie to him. "I don't regret last night," I finally admit, my voice so low I'm not sure if he even hears me.

"Why did you run out of the room this morning?"

I shrug. It isn't something I can answer because I don't know the answer myself.

"Darryn, if we want this to work, I need you to be able to talk to me."

Have this work? What does he mean, is he talking about this so-called marriage? That brings my eyes up to his. For a moment I would have sworn I read something in his eyes, maybe this is a little more than just a protection detail for him.

"What do you want me to tell you, Bryce? I was scared and confused. Everything happened so fast yesterday, and when that alarm went off this morning I realized it wasn't all a dream and it terrified me for a moment."

"Darryn, I understand everything was a whirlwind yesterday, but if I pressured you at any point last night, I'm sorry." Bryce stands up and backs away from me.

He is misunderstanding what I am saying. How do I explain it without telling him how I feel? Before I can try and explain myself, he walks away and heads down the hall to his room. He just walked away from this. He didn't give me a chance to explain. I hear a door close and my heart sinks. I can't sit here and let him think he pressured me into anything

146

last night, that isn't fair to him, and I can't keep running from things.

Walking down the hall, I knock on his bedroom door. "Bryce, can we talk?"

He doesn't respond, so I knock again. "Bryce, please talk to me."

Still nothing! I'm not going to let him go to bed thinking he did something wrong last night. Opening the door, I realize he isn't in here. The shower is on in the bathroom and my whole body heats instantly, thinking of him naked and wet. Flashes of last night run through my head and an ache starts in my core. Before I can talk myself out of something I hope I don't regret, I quickly undress, leaving my clothes in a pile on the floor. I take a deep breath and open the bathroom door. Steam rushes out, hitting me in the face. I can see the silhouette of him in the shower, and my fear is now completely gone and replaced by a need for him. All I can think about now is having his wet body pressed to mine, that's what gets my feet to move.

Opening the shower door, Bryce doesn't turn around. He has his hands braced against the wall and his head hanging down, water cascading over his head. Stepping inside, I shut the door and wrap my arms around his waist, pressing my front up against his back. I feel his body tense, but he doesn't move or say a word.

Ducking under one of his arms, I bring myself to stand in front of him. His arms drop away and his head comes up, but he doesn't touch me. He isn't even looking at me, he is looking up over my head. Bringing my hand up to the back of his head, I force him to look me in the eye and that's when I see it...fear.

"I'm sorry, Bryce, you misunderstood me, or maybe I was just not explaining it right." I realize I can't let him go on thinking he did something wrong last night, or pressured me into something I wasn't ready and willing for, not with him knowing my past.

The questioning look is all I get. He is only touching me because I have pressed my body against his, which he is affected by, I can feel the proof against my belly. But other than that, nothing.

"I'm not upset by what happened last night with you. I wanted it just as much as you did and it was great, that's not what scared me this morning. Being held by you all night and waking up to you this morning scared the hell out of me not because of what we did leading up to it, but coming to realize what was happening to me after everything."

"What does that even mean, Darryn?" Finally, he speaks!

I can't back down from this now, if he decides after this that we need to figure out different living arrangements for Kendall and I then so be it. "Bryce, I'm starting to have feelings for you and that is scaring the hell out of me." There, it is out and in the open now.

Nothing in his facial features change, he just stands there staring down at me while water runs over the both of us. I can't tell what he is thinking, if he is mad, relieved, confused, nothing. I can't breathe and I feel the tears start to burn the back of my eyes. Looking down at his chest, I try to catch my breath, push back the tears and when I think I have myself collected, I look back up at him and that's when I see it. His eyes are changing color, to that crystal, almost clear green they get right before he is going to kiss me, and I act before I can think twice.

My hands go up and into his wet hair and I press his head down to mine, taking his lips in a demanding kiss. His arms instantly go around my waist pressing us together, it isn't enough for me though. I need him inside of me, I ache for it.

Bryce presses me up against the shower wall, lifting me up, his lips devouring mine. I wrap my legs around his waist, now feeling his hardness against my center.

"I need you inside of me, Bryce, please," I beg, not wanting to wait any longer.

Bryce moves away just enough to get his hand between us, placing himself just inside of me. I can't wait any longer so I press myself down onto him, feeling every inch of him slide deep inside. We both moan and with his hands circling my waist on both sides, he sets the rhythm. The cool shower tiles pressed against my back and with Bryce's hot, wet body moving against my front, and his hardness filling me completely on the inside, it is more than I can take. My release comes fast and hard, causing me to scream out his name against his lips. My body tightens around him, he thrusts one last time into me hard and I feel his body release. He bites into my lower lip which just heightens my release. His lips move down to my neck and he mumbles something but I can't hear what it is.

Bryce slowly pulls himself out of me and I want to scream no. I'm not ready to have this feeling end. Sitting me down on my feet, Bryce reaches around and turns off the water.

"The water is getting cold and I'm not done with you yet." He grabs my hand and leads me out of the shower.

I hadn't even noticed the cold water, my body is on fire at the moment, and it doesn't help that he just told me he isn't finished yet. We don't even dry off, he leads me out to the bedroom and over to his bed. Turning me around, he pushes me down onto the cool sheets, taking my breath away feeling their coolness against my skin. Bryce pushes my shoulders back so that I am now laying back on the bed, my leg hanging over the side. I watch as he kneels down on the ground in front of me. His eyes never leave mine, I have myself braced by my elbows behind me. With his hands on my knees, he separates my legs. He kisses the inside of one thigh and with those clear green eyes looking straight at me, his tongue dips into my now very hot and wet core. My arms are shaking so bad, they won't hold me any longer. I fall back against the bed, my hands going into Bryce's hair, pressing him closer into me. I can feel another release coming, but I don't want to give into it just yet.

"Bryce, please," I beg, not knowing what for as I push him away from me. All I know is I don't want this to end that fast.

He crawls up, his body rubbing in all the right ways against mine, and his lips claim one nipple. My hand traces down his side and finds his hardness between us. I slowly stroke down and then up, with each stroke he sucks that much harder on my nipple. I want to scream, but hold it in. I run my finger over his tip, feeling the wetness starting to bead. He is close.

His lips suck hard one last time on my nipple and then move up to my lips. "I need to be inside you again, Darryn, I can't seem to get enough of you."

Before I can respond, or maybe I should say beg him to take me, he stands up and flips me over, my front side now on the mattress and my feet on the floor. His hand caresses my backside for a moment, I wiggle myself against him and I hear him moan. I spread my legs just a little further apart and arch my back, begging him to take me now.

He enters me with one thrust, and my breath rushes out of me. With his hands on my hips, I feel him pull almost all the way out and then thrust back in with a rush. His hand snakes around and one finger slides inside my folds and that is when I lose everything. He thrusts deep inside of me one last time, and I bury my face into the mattress to muffle my scream as we find our release together. It is so intense my legs give out and all I can do is lay face down on the bed, Bryce's body covering me up and his heavy breath in my ear.

CHAPTER TWENTY-TWO

Bryce

I'm not sure of what just happened. One minute I'm taking a shower feeling like an asshole and swearing to never touch Darryn again, and the next I have her pinned up against the shower wall. As if that isn't enough, I think I basically dragged her out of the bathroom, pushed her down onto my bed and enjoyed yet another amazing experience with this amazing woman. Now here we are in my bed, naked, Darryn draped half across me, her head resting on my chest and I can't think of too much that would make me get up from this spot. On the other side of it, we do need to talk.

"Are you awake?" I ask.

"Hmmm," is all the answer I get back from her.

"Darryn, I know you're tired, but I don't want the same

reaction out of you tomorrow morning when the alarm clock goes off as you had this morning, we need to talk about this."

She takes a deep breath and I wait. After a moment, she re-adjusts her arms so that they are crossed over my chest and she rests her chin on her hands, looking up at me. "I'm sorry about this morning, Bryce. I'm sorry about the whole day; however, I'm not sorry about last night or tonight." She gives me a sleepy smile.

"I guess my question is, are we going to have a repeat in the morning like today?"

"Tonight when you asked me why I ran out of the room this morning, my answer came out wrong. I was scared, yes, but not for the reasons you were thinking. Last night was great and I don't regret it, as well as what just happened." She takes a deep breath and then looks away from me.

"Hey, talk to me." I push a piece of hair off her forehead.

"Bryce, I'm starting to have feelings for you." She repeats what she told me earlier in the shower.

I'm not sure how to respond to her though. I'm happy she is opening up, but now I have to be careful on what I say. I love this woman and her daughter and there is nothing that would make me happier than to have her love me back, but that isn't what she is saying right now. She is admitting to having some feelings for me, it's not a confession of love, but it's a start and it gives me a little hope that this may all work out.

"And because you are starting to have these feelings is why you ran out of bed this morning?" I decide to tread slow on this subject, basically my plan is to follow her lead.

She nods her head, looking a little shy, which I find to be cute. "Look, Darryn, if we are being honest here, I will have to admit that you and Kendall have started to burrow your ways into my heart as well, but I would hope that you know that. I just married you! Do you think I offer that to all the women I'm trying to protect from their crazy ex-boyfriends?"

"How many woman have you had to protect from their ex-boyfriends?" she asks.

"Well, I will say you aren't the first, but you are the first that I have offered to move into my house and then marry the next day." I smile down at her.

"I guess that answers my next question of if I was going to have to watch my back for any crazy exes of yours."

"Look, I want you to be able to talk to me, Darryn, to be honest with me when something isn't feeling right to you. I don't want you to run and hide from me, that's not going to work too well."

Crawling her way up my body, Darryn is now eye to eye with me. "I promise and again, I'm sorry for today."

Reaching up, I bury my fingers into her hair at the back of her head and bring her lips down to mine. "Can I be honest about one other thing?" I ask before taking her lips with mine.

She nods, our lips brushing against each other's.

"I kind of like sharing my bed with you. How do you feel about just agreeing on it now so that way there is no more confusion about it in the future? Also, I was going to offer this before but didn't want you freaking out on me, but I have a whole other closet that is empty next to mine. It's yours if you want to put your clothes in there instead of trying to find room for both yours and Kendall's clothes in the spare room closet."

"Wow, it sounds like you are asking me to move into your room." She smiles down at me.

"Well, you are my wife." I put my finger through the ring that is hanging from her neck and show it to her as a reminder.

"Then I have the rights as your wife to do this." She kisses me and rubs her body up and down against mine.

"Anytime you would like, no complaints from me."

It's amazing how time flies when you are having fun, right? Summer is here, and the last couple of months have been uneventful in the subject of Brett. Darryn keeps asking if she can drive herself to work and take Kendall back to daycare. She says she doesn't want to wear out my mother. I think my mom will have more issues with not being able to watch her. Tonight, we have decided to go to the carnival that is going on down at the beach just for a little fun and relaxation, we have both been very busy with work.

We are standing at one of the ball throwing games when I hear familiar voices coming up behind us. Turning around, I see my sister, Charliee, along with her best friend, Jayden, her boyfriend, Travis, and another guy who I have not met yet.

"Looks like my sister is here," I say over to Darryn as I watch the group approach us.

Darryn's hand goes to her chest, she is checking to see if her ring is tucked into her shirt. She does that all the time when we are around other people, she absolutely doesn't want people to know what is going on between the two of us. Every time she does it my heart skips a little. I know it's crazy and I know I promised her I wouldn't say anything to anyone, but it is killing me. I've never deliberately stayed away from my brother and sister as much as I have the last couple of months. Not that I'm trying to hide Darryn from them, but I know the more we are together, things may come out. It's hard enough working with Derrick and not having things slip around him.

My sister is a lot more observant, she will know I am hiding something.

Charliee walks straight up to me and hugs me. "Hey, I didn't know you were coming tonight."

I don't get a chance to say anything in return, Charliee's attention goes straight to Darryn. "Hi, I'm Charliee, Bryce's sister."

They shake hands. "I'm Darryn and this is my daughter, Kendall."

Charliee glances at me quickly with a little smirk before she bends down and says hello to Kendall who is sitting in her stroller.

Well, everyone is here, I figure I better make the introductions. "That's Travis, Charliee's boyfriend. That's Jayden, her best friend." I look over at the other guy and stop, I have no clue who he is.

"I'm Cameron." He extends his hand out to me and then to Darryn.

I'm going to assume this is Jayden's boyfriend.

It's nice to meet you guys." Darryn smiles at them all.

"So how did you guys meet?" My sister goes straight into the questions.

Darryn looks over at me, giving me an uncertain look. I'm not sure if it's because she doesn't want to tell Charliee how we met, or because she isn't sure how much to tell her.

I clear my throat. "We actually met the night of the explosion. Darryn was the paramedic who took care of you, Charliee."

The light in my sister's eyes fades for a moment. She has been doing great. She was able to go back to work teaching at the deaf school for the last month or so of the school year, and now that she is dating Travis, who I believe is moving in with her, Derrick and I have been needed a lot less. Which I have mixed feelings about. Derrick and I are used to having her back, checking up on her. Even though she swears she is good and she does have Levi, her hearing dog, we always worry about her. Now she doesn't need us and that is hard to stand aside and swallow as well. However, with everything going on with Darryn right now, it is working out for me.

Charliee quickly recovers her smile. "Well then, I guess I should be thanking you." She is still knelt down in front of Kendall and her eyes redirect back to her, she is hiding.

"Not at all. I'm just happy to know you have fully recovered."

Charliee smiles up at us once more. "Everyone here had a part in that."

Charliee goes to stand back up and Levi lunges forward, knocking Charliee off balance and she falls forward, almost landing in Kendall's lap. She manages to redirect herself to fall to the side of the stroller, not into it.

Charliee pulls back tight on Levi's leash. "Levi, what's your problem? Sit!"

Travis helps Charliee up. I look over at Levi. He isn't pulling any longer, I think he has realized what he just did, but his ears are up and alert, and there is a low growl coming from him. "What's wrong with him? He never acts like this," I ask as I look in the direction Levi is looking.

My senses are on alert now. Levi is very well trained, he would never lunge at someone, or chance injuring Charliee, or try and leave her. "What's wrong with him, he never acts like this?"

Levi starts to pull again. Travis takes the leash from Charliee's hand and pulls back on Levi. "He did this earlier, but I just brushed it off thinking something spooked him," Travis explains, but he too is now looking around, more alert.

"Oh my God." Charliee's voice brings my attention back to her. She is ghost white and shaking.

Jayden is the first to ask, "Charliee, what's wrong?"

She doesn't answer, but starts to shake more violently. Travis shoves Levi's leash into my hands as his attention goes to Charliee.

"Charliee, talk to us." Travis is now standing right in front of her.

Charliee points over in the direction of one of the little kids' rides. "That's the guy from the restaurant, the one who ran into me outside. He is standing there in the blue jeans and plaid a shirt, and he's wearing a backpack."

We all follow the direction Charliee is pointing and Levi begins to bark now. I can barely hold him back. The man Charliee pointed out turns around, I'm sure Levi's barking is getting his attention. The moment he realizes it is directed at him and we are all staring at him, he takes off running.

I shove Levi's leash into Jayden's hand. "Call 911, let them know what's going on. You guys get out of here now," I yell back as I take off in the direction the guy ran.

I can see the back of the guy but there are so many people around and he keeps weaving in and out of my sight. The man has a backpack, that alone is putting me on high alert. If this is the man, he has already set off two bombs—one at the restaurant where Charliee was involved and one in a movie theater. If he sets one off here, the number of causalities would be way too great, and my family is still here.

I pass a security guard and pull out my badge. "I'm a police officer, we have a possible bomb situation. Please start getting this place cleared out and call it in, tell them Bryce Brooksman had you call and is in pursuit."

I shoot everything off at the man and hope he takes me seriously. I don't even wait to see if he is following my directions, I don't want to lose the man. I turn the corner I swear I saw him go around and swear out loud. I am met with a rush of people being evacuated from the area.

Stopping, I look around. This would be a perfect chance for him to blend in and get himself out.

"Bryce, where did he go?" Travis comes up behind me, Cameron next to him.

"Where's the girls?" I ask, now concerned no one is with them.

"Don't worry, they are on their way out to the parking lot all together," Travis explains.

"Where is the asshole?" Cameron asks, looking around at all the people rushing around us.

"I don't know, I've lost him in the crowd," I answer back, looking around.

"What do you mean you lost him? He got away? Are you kidding me?!" Cameron yells next to me, taking me by surprise a little.

I look over at him with a questioning look. I get it, I want the man caught as well, but why is he getting so mad at me? "Hey, they are evacuating everyone, I lost him in the crowd." I have no idea why I'm defending myself to this guy.

Travis puts a hand on my shoulder. "Bryce, it's all right, he doesn't mean it that way. You see, Cameron's parents were both killed in the bombing that Charliee was involved in."

"Shit." What are the odds of that? I'm in shock, this guy probably wants this crazy guy worse than I do. "I'm sorry, man."

"No, I'm sorry, I shouldn't have snapped at you. Let's just look for him." Cameron won't look at me and before I can respond with something back, he takes off into the crowd.

This is going to be like looking for "a needle in a haystack" as they say. I didn't even get a good look at the man's face, by now he could have easily taken off his shirt, ditched the backpack and is blending in with the crowd enough to get out of the area. This is pretty much a useless search, but I will look until everyone has cleared and we have checked all areas.

CHAPTER TWENTY-THREE

Darryn

I decide to bring Kendall back home instead of sitting in the parking lot with Charliee and Jayden. If a bomb did go off, I didn't want her anywhere near the area. Luckily I had the car keys in my purse.

It's a little strange, I have been asking Bryce for weeks now if I can drive my own car to work, put Kendall back in daycare, get back to a little bit of a normal life, but right now I'm not sure if it's from the events of tonight or what, but I am on edge. I feel like I need to keep a solid eye on my rear-view mirror to make sure no one is following us. I think I'm just paranoid, but I hate the feeling all the same. Once we pull into the driveway, I grab Kendall out of the car quickly and basically run up to the front door. My hands are shaking so bad I drop the keys trying to unlock the door.

"Mommy, okay?" Kendall asks as I bend over to pick them up.

I take a deep breath and tell myself to calm down, Kendall is starting to pick up on my uneasiness and I don't want that. "Yes, honey, Mommy is fine." I smile at her.

Walking inside, I sit Kendall down and quickly lock the door. "Let's go put your pajamas on and Mommy will turn a movie on for you in your room."

I usually read her to sleep but tonight I am too on edge. I know if I put the movie on, it won't take long for her to fall asleep. Plus she will think it's a treat, that'll make me feel a little better about skipping out on our nightly routine.

Looking up at the clock for what feels like the thousandth time, it's almost midnight and I haven't heard anything from Bryce. I don't want to call him and bother him if they have the guy in custody, but I will feel so much better when he is home.

My phone buzzes next to me causing me to jump. Looking down at it, I see Bryce's name and pic on the screen. "Hello."

"Hey, can you unlock the door for me? Derrick is dropping me off now."

He sounds exhausted. I want to ask if they got the guy, but I don't. I'll wait until he gets into the house, or maybe tomorrow.

Getting up, I go and unlock the door, relief flooding through me when I open it and see Bryce getting out of Derrick's car. I want to run out and throw myself into his arms, but I keep myself at the front door. They talk for a moment, Bryce turns around and waves at me, then turns back to his brother. I know they are talking about me.

Finally, Bryce shuts the car door and starts for the front door. He looks tired and defeated. That can't be good. Even exhausted, if he would have caught the guy, I would expect to see some happiness in his eyes. His walk is even dragging.

He stops in front of me at the door but doesn't say anything. I have an urge to wrap my arms around him and just hug him. I find that I want to be in his arms just as much, pressed against his body knowing everything is all right.

Grabbing his hand, I pull him into the house and shut the door. Once it's locked, I wrap my arms around his waist and we both just stand here in the entry way of the house, just holding each other.

"I'm going to guess you guys didn't get the guy." I speak against his chest, breaking the silence between the two of us.

Bryce pulls away from me and I instantly feel empty. I follow him as he moves over to the couch and sits down. "No, we didn't get him. We are thinking he was able to use the crowd when the place was being evacuated to sneak out. To top it off, I found out tonight Cameron's parents were both killed in the same bombing that Charliee was involved in."

"Wow, really?" What are the odds of that happening?

"How is Kendall?"

"She's fine. Asleep. She went down pretty easy, I'm sure it helped that I let her go to sleep with a movie on."

Bryce looks over at me, he is searching for something. "Are you all right?"

"Of course, why are you asking?"

"You always read her to sleep. You get upset when my mom tells you she allowed her to go to bed watching a movie," he points out.

Shrugging, I look down at my hands.

"Darryn, talk to me, what's going through that beautiful mind of yours?"

I don't want to tell him about how jumpy I've been since he wasn't with us, but I find that I open up to him even if I don't want to. He usually figures it all out anyway so why try and hide it?

"I don't know, I think with everything that happened tonight I am just on edge."

"Did anything happen on the way home?" Concern etches his voice. Like he doesn't have enough to be worried about already.

"No, nothing happened. Like I said, I think it's just everything that happened tonight has my nerves on alert. I will say, you won't have to worry about me begging you to allow me to drive to work alone any longer, or to put Kendall back in daycare. My imagination tonight took care of all of that for you." I hate to admit it though.

Again, Bryce just studies me for a moment. "You aren't hiding anything, right, Darryn? You would tell me if something happened or if he tried to contact you, right?"

I am nodding as he is asking. "I have no reason to keep any of that from you, Bryce. I hope you know that. I know what you have given up to protect Kendall and myself. I may want some independence back, but not that way. Like I said, I'm not even going to fight you on that either anymore."

I look up at him and could have sworn I saw a flash of anger or maybe irritation cross his face. Why, I don't understand. I just told him I won't keep begging him to let me start doing things alone any longer. I thought that would make him happy, or at least relieved.

"I'm going to head to bed." Bryce stands up from the

couch and starts for the hallway. He stops and looks over his shoulder at me. "Are you coming?"

I want to ask why he all of a sudden seems upset with me, but I see the exhaustion in his eyes and I decide to let it go for now. Maybe I am just imagining things. Getting up, I follow him to the room, nothing else is said between us.

"All right, it's time for you to start talking to me, Darryn. What is going on with you? I've been waiting and hoping you would start talking on your own, but nothing. Are you having problems with the ex and no one is telling me?"

Tom and I have just finished our shift, I shut the door from getting out of rig and he turns to me and goes off. It takes me by surprise. "What do you mean, Tom? Nothing has happened, why would you think it has? Plus, don't you think if it had, Bryce would have told you?"

"Then what's going on with you? The last couple of weeks you haven't been yourself."

It's been two weeks since we were at the fair and Charliee recognized the man from the night of the bombing. Since that night, Bryce hasn't been the same. He still spoils Kendall and myself, if I am being honest. We are still sharing a bed, and still having sex, but something has changed since that night, I just can't figure out what. I want to ask him, but I haven't.

"I think everything is just getting to me. It's been how long now and Brett hasn't shown up anywhere. I keep wondering if I just imagined everything to begin with. It's crazy that you still have to take time out of your day to follow me back to the station after every shift. I'm starting to think this is all for nothing and just let everyone get back to their normal lives."

My heart sinks as the words come out of my mouth. Sure,

that would mean Tom wouldn't have to be my personal body-guard after work any longer, and Kendall could get back to daycare which would give Bryce's mom a break. It would also mean I would have to let Bryce go. More than once the thought has crossed my mind that he is getting tired of this farce of a marriage and that's what has changed between us. I wonder if he thinks that I have made everything up and now he is stuck in a marriage.

"Come on, Darryn, talk to me. I see the wheels turning in your head, there is something you aren't telling me." Tom's words break through my thoughts.

I can't talk to him about all of this. No one knows we are married except Bryce's parents. I had him promise me he wouldn't tell his brother and sister. We have never talked about how that is for him but I know it rips him apart keeping this from them. Not only him but his parents are keeping it from them as well. How can I sit here and tell Tom and basi-cally beg Bryce to not tell his family?

"Really, Tom, I think it's just me getting into my own head. If Brett is around I wish he would just show himself and we can be done with all of this. If he isn't, then maybe it's time for me to get back to my normal life. Find my own apartment, give you and Bryce back your lives."

"I think you need to talk to Bryce about all of this. I'm pretty sure he will feel the same way as I do and believe it's not worth taking the risk."

"So how long do we all go on like this?" My voice raises. Quickly I look away from Tom, I can feel the tears burning the back of my eyes.

Damn Brett, he is still controlling my life without being anywhere near me. I need to get over him and the fear. There have been times when I have spotted someone in a crowd and had to look twice thinking it was him. I'm paranoid and I need to move past it, he may have finally given up on trying to find me. The note in my apartment the day it was broken into was the only thing that kept me believing he had found me. I haven't even shown it to Bryce, I almost threw it away, but decided against it and hid it in a pair of shoes I never wear.

"Hey, sorry! I didn't mean to upset you." Tom apologizes and that tears at me even more.

This man has done so much for me through all of this and what do I do? Yell at him. "Tom, I'm sorry. You have no idea what it means to me to have you do all that you are. I'm just ready for it all to be over, but that's no excuse to yell at you. Please forgive me."

"Don't worry about me, it's going to take a lot more then you yelling a little at me to make me upset. I understand, Darryn, I just want you to know I'm here if you need someone to talk to."

I give my best effort of a smile. Without anything else to say I head to my car, knowing that Tom will go to his and follow me back to the station, like every other day.

Tom talks to Bryce for a little bit before he heads for home after following me to the station. I go straight to Bryce's car and get in with only a wave to Tom. I figure Tom is telling about our conversation and right now, I don't care. When we get home, I am going to talk to Bryce about all of this. If Tom is noticing something was wrong then maybe it was time for Bryce and me to talk, figure out what's next.

I watch as the two of them shake hands. Bryce pulls his phone out of his pocket but I can't tell from here if he is making a call or receiving one. He ends it before he opens the door to the car.

"Hey," he says as he sits down and closes the driver's side door.

"Hey," is all I say back and then look once again out of the passenger side window, my chest hurting.

I wonder for a moment if I should just keep things the way they are, but what would that fix? Is it really that fair for me to keep Bryce in a marriage that was only created to keep my daughter and me safe? My heart may be breaking over the thought of leaving him and moving on with our own lives, but it's what's fair to Bryce. I owe him that with everything he has done for us.

I realize we aren't headed in the direction of his parents' house, but to his house. "Do we need to do something else before we pick up Kendall?"

He shakes his head, but says nothing.

"All right, then where are we going?"

"Home! Mom has agreed to keep Kendall for the night."

What the hell?! Well, now I know who he was on the phone with. "Why do you think it's all right for you to make that kind of decision without asking me? She is my child, not yours." My words are harsh and I know it, but right now I am pissed.

I see his face drop a little, but he quickly recovers it. "We have things we need to talk about and I'm going to make sure I have your full attention, and this way you have no excuse to hide from it."

What did Tom tell him? I know trying to argue with him is a waste of time, so I just sit back, cross my arms over my chest and sit in silence for the rest of the drive back to the house.

Once we pull into the driveway, I quickly jump out of the car, my keys in hand, and go into the house. Bryce follows right behind me, shutting the door behind us.

"All right, what the hell is going on? And don't tell me nothing." The words are out of his mouth the second the door clicks shut.

We are standing in the living room and from the stance Bryce is taking, we aren't going any further until we talk. Maybe this is a good thing. I'm pissed at the moment which will make it a lot easier for me to tell him what I have been thinking and not hold anything back.

"Tom tells me you are thinking about moving out."

Out of everything Tom could have told Bryce, that is what this is about. Not that I am worried I had imagined all of this, or that I thought Brett has given up way too much, but that I was moving out. "That's not exactly what I said."

"All right, then tell me, Darryn, what exactly did you say?"

I have never really seen Bryce mad at me, not like this at least. It's strange, when Brett was mad at me I wanted to run and hide, my stomach would feel heavy with not knowing what he was going to do. I didn't trust him. With Bryce it is completely different. I don't want to run and I'm not scared. I know Bryce wouldn't do anything that would hurt, at least not intentionally. That's when it hits me, I am completely in love with this man and I need to let him go.

Taking a deep breath and fighting back the tears, my heart is feeling like it is being pulled apart into two pieces. "Bryce, we haven't heard anything, or seen anything since the night I thought I was being followed. Maybe it was all just my imagination."

I'm not about to tell him about the note left at my apartment that day. He would never let me go if he knew about it. That night Brett was in my apartment and he wanted me to know about it.

"Darryn, I'm not ready to assume that. Yours and Kendall's safety is way too important to me to chance that."

"Bryce, you have totally turned your life upside down for my daughter and me. Not only that, but Tom has to get home later at night because he has to follow me around. It's not fair to anyone."

"I asked Tom about all of this at the beginning. He is actually the one who offered. I only asked him to make sure he was with you during working hours."

That warms my heart. Tom is a great friend, but it still isn't fair. "Bryce, I'm done depending on everyone, I need to get on with my life and you guys with yours. You should be concentrating on the bomber, taking care of your family, not worrying about mine."

Bryce just stares at me. I can tell he wants to say something but what, I have no idea. "Look, I work tomorrow, I think I will go and pick up Kendall from your mom's after work, without Tom following me, and then after tomorrow Kendall will go back to daycare. I have this weekend off, so if you don't mind us hanging out here until then, I will look for an apartment."

"You're my wife, Darryn!"

He surprises me a little. It's like he is trying to convince me to stay. He even said when this was all discussed that after it was all over we would be parting paths. I have to admit, my heart jumps a little with hope that just maybe he will want me to stay, that he has started to feel for me as I have for him.

"Bryce, you married me to keep me safe, I can't keep allowing you to put your life on hold anymore."

His arms are folded across his chest and he is just staring at me. I shift back and forth on my feet, wanting to just run and hide in Kendall's room. All he would have to do is tell me he cares for me. I wouldn't even need to hear that he loves me, just knowing this is more than a protection detail would make me stay.

"Look, I think it's best if I sleep in the spare room with Kendall for the next couple of nights." I need some space and time to think. Plus, each night I'm in his arms is another night I fall that much deeper for him.

CHAPTER TWENTY-FOUR

Bryce

I know the last few weeks things have been a little strung tight between the two of us. I want to talk to her about it but always talk myself out of it. Now look where that has gotten us, Darryn is talking about moving out. It's the last thing I want. I was hoping, and to be honest I thought, I had seen a little side of her that may have started to care a little more for me, but obviously I was wrong. I want to tell her that I have fallen in love with her, but I don't think she will believe me on that right now. She would think I am just telling her that to get her to stay.

I don't think the threat of her ex is her imagination. I have no idea why he is waiting so long to appear again, and maybe he has been around the whole time. We have been careful not to have Darryn alone. I have done everything I can think of to make sure he couldn't follow her to my house or my parents. He may just be waiting for us to slip up, and Darryn and Kendall moving out could be that slip up.

Now she wants to sleep in the spare room. I can't even imagine not having her next to me at night anymore. I know words aren't going to keep her here, and I have a couple days to convince her to stay. One thing is for sure, she isn't sleeping in Kendall's room.

"Look, I can't stop you if this is what you want to do. I will help you with whatever you need and I hope you always know that you have me if you need me, but as for the part of sleeping with Kendall..." I close the space in between us and wrap an arm around her waist. Bringing my head down to hers I stop, our lips almost touching. I can feel her warm breath and it takes all the strength I have not to claim those lips, and then beg her to love me like I love her. "It's not happening. If all I have are a couple more nights with you, than I want you wrapped around me, and me deep inside of you every minute that we can."

Darryn takes a sharp intake of breath and her eyes go wide. I may not be able to tell her how I feel, but I plan to show her as much as possible, with a small sliver of hope that she will change her mind before this weekend. I'm not going to let her go, I just need to convince her of that.

I don't want to give her time to argue with me and decide to use her surprise to my advantage. I claim her lips before she can say another word. If there is one thing I know for sure, it is the chemistry between the two us. I feel her hands go to my chest and I wait for her to push against me. It will be difficult but I will let her go. I never want her to feel like she is being pressured with me. But instead of pushing me away, each hand grabs a fist full of my shirt and holds on. That's all the answer I need. Picking her up, I cradle her in my arms, my lips never leaving hers. Quickly I walk down the hallway and into our room, sitting her down on our bed.

She looks up at me. I know she is battling with this, and I will stop if she tells me to. "You aren't going to make this very easy for me, are you?"

Her question surprises me a little. I'm not the one who has decided she needs to move out. From the look in her eyes I would say it's the last thing she wants to do. That gives me a little hope that convincing her may not be as difficult as I thought it might be. I need to show her how much she means to me, I need to prove it. Words aren't going to be enough with her, they never have been.

I need her to make the next move. To know this is want she wants. We stare at each other for a few moments and I know she is battling with herself. Here we are, her sitting on the bed looking up at me, and all I can do is stand here looking back at her waiting.

Her hands finally come up to my stomach and she gently pushes me back so that she can stand. My heart drops, she is going to walk away from me and I'm going to have to let her. Shutting my eyes for a moment, I have to fight the urge to shake her. How does she not know my feelings? I may not have voiced them but I know I have for damn sure shown them.

"Bryce, open your eyes." Her voice is low.

Opening them, my heart stops. A single tear is rolling down her cheek. With my thumb I wipe it away and fight the urge to pull her into my arms and just hold her.

"I don't want to sleep anywhere else than in your arms." Her words shock me, but what confuses me more is the fact that more tears are rolling down her cheeks now and she looks sad.

"I know I have to let you go, it's the only fair thing for you," she continues, and my heart sinks once again. She is still planning on leaving me and now all I am is more confused than before.

"Darryn, you don't have to let me go..." She stops me before I can tell her that I love her. Screw all my thoughts before, she needs to know.

"Bryce, I've already made up my mind and nothing you say is going to change that, but I'm not ready to let go of you yet. I know this is unfair to ask, but I need to be with you until that time, that is if you want me."

I have a huge urge to shake her again. Then I realize nothing is going to change this stubborn woman's mind and right now, I just need her. I will figure out a way to make her see what she means to me, but for now I will let her think I'm giving into her.

"I'm yours, Darryn, for as long as you want me." With my hand at the back of her head, my fingers digging into her thick hair, I claim her lips once again.

Darryn's body crushes against mine and her arms go up over my shoulder, her fingers now in my hair. Neither one of us wants to let go, which gives me a spark of hope. I love this woman more than words can express and I will get her to see that.

My fingers relax in her hair and I slow the intensity of the kiss down. I don't want this fast, I want it to be something that makes her think, something she has never experienced before. I don't want to have sex with Darryn, I want to make love to her.

Moving my hands down to the bottom of her work shirt, I

slide my hands up and bring the shirt up and over her head, only separating our lips to move the shirt past them. Trailing my hands back down her arms, my hands span each side of her waist, squeezing slightly, pulling her hips tighter against mine.

I hear a low moan escape her. "I want your shirt off, Bryce. I need to feel your skin against mine."

Who am I to argue with her? I stand in front of her and allow her to work my shirt up my chest and over my head, it lands on the floor next to where hers fell. I watch as she then reaches behind her back and she removes her own bra. Her hands then start at my biceps and trace a path up and around my neck, her nails now lightly scraping my scalp, our bodies pressed against each other. She pulls my head down and kisses me.

I bring one hand up, brushing my fingers against one very tight nipple. Trailing kisses down her neck, I finally reach her nipple with my lips, lightly kissing the hard bud. Just that one slight touch and Darryn's knees buckle, her arms tightening around my neck to hold herself up. Pushing her back, she sits down first on the bed, and with a slight push from me, she lays back.

Before joining her, I strip out of my remaining clothes, her eyes watching my every move. Now that I'm standing before her completely naked, all I can think about is her entire body naked against mine. Her nipples are tight and begging to be touched, so with each hand I cup a breast and squeeze slightly, then tug lightly on each nipple. Her eyes close, her head goes back and her back arches, thrusting her chest out to me, begging me for more.

My hands now travel down to the waist of her pants and I slowly pull them and any remaining clothing down her legs.

Bending down, I start at her knee and start trailing small kisses up her thigh. My eyes never leave her face, I like watching her reactions to what I'm doing to her. Her eyes are closed, her hands clutching the sheets on the bed. The higher I go, the more my body pushes her legs apart. I tease her a little more as I blow on her heated core. I'm rewarded with another moan. Ever so lightly, I lick up her outer folds and then trail my tongue up over her belly, her ribs and then finally to one tight and begging nipple. Sucking it fully into my mouth, my hand covering the other, my name fills the room. Darryn's legs wrap around my waist, which almost causes me to lose all control once I feel her hot, very wet center on my hardness, but I'm not done with her yet.

Darryn, using her hands, presses my head down, which is my sign to suck a little harder, nibble a little more on the nipple, and pinch a little harder on the other. Between the little sounds Darryn is making, and her body rubbing hot and wet against mine, I am about to lose my mind.

I move my one hand from her breast and down to her heated center. Teasing between her folds, I find her just as wet as she is hot. Leaving her breast, my lips trail kisses up her neck and claim her lips once again.

"Please, Bryce, I need you," Darryn begs.

"Darryn, I need you," I say as I take myself and enter her slowly, causing us both to moan this time.

I will never get enough of being inside this amazing woman. Her body tightens around me, pulling me in even deeper as her legs tighten around my waist like she is afraid to let go. Pulling out, I can feel just my tip inside of her, and when her body shivers I almost lose myself completely. I thrust deep inside of her once again. I repeat the motion again and again, each time a little faster and a little harder. I can feel her body beginning to quake around me, each time tightening her around me more and more. I'm not sure how much longer I am going to be able to hold back.

"Darryn, please." I now find myself begging her.

That's all it takes, again my name fills the room, and I'm pretty sure hers escapes from my lips as together we find our release. Feeling her body pull me in deeper and deeper, all I can do is hold her tight and listen to both of us trying to breathe.

I'm not going to let her go! Somehow, some way, I will get her to stay with me! For now, I just need to convince her to allow things to stay the way they are so that I don't worry about her while trying to convince her and on top of that, work right now is crazy with trying to catch the bomber.

Since that night at the carnival, Derrick and I have worked nonstop trying to figure out more about this guy.

"Hey, are you awake?" I whisper in Darryn's ear.

She doesn't say anything, just nods her head. She has her head laying on my chest so I can't see her eyes.

"Can I ask you a favor?"

This question brings her eyes up to mine with her head tilted back, now resting on my shoulder.

"I know you said tomorrow you wanted to start driving yourself to work and taking Kendall back to the daycare, but I want to ask that you wait on that. You asked to give you until this weekend so I'm asking the same thing. Plus, it gives me some time to break the news to my mom, she is going to be lost without Kendall." I try to lighten the mood.

"Bryce, I don't want Tom to have to worry about me any longer. I know your mom and dad love Kendall, she loves them and I'm not trying to take her away from them, but I feel bad about turning everyone's lives upside down."

"Tom is going to worry about you regardless if he has to be there to follow you or not. You are the only one who thinks Brett isn't around, just for your information. As for my parents, trust me, you didn't turn their lives upside down, you gave my mom a grandchild to spoil and she is enjoying the hell out of it."

She looks away from me again. She does this when she doesn't want me figuring out what she is thinking. She seems to believe I can read her mind. That talent isn't needed with someone who tells you everything with their eyes.

Shifting us around, I place her under me so that she can't hide from me as I tower over her. "Darryn, please do this for me."

Her eyes soften and I see tears start to well up, I have to hide my shock. It's at this moment I realize she cares for me, I can see it. This is why she hides from me, she doesn't want me to see it. Finally, she nods her agreement to my request.

"I'm going to make you see it," I state with a smile on my face.

She gives me a puzzled look. "See what?"

"How much you mean to me."

Her eyes go wide and I hear her sharp intake of breath. I don't give her a chance to argue with me or question it. I claim her lips and for the second time tonight, we make love.

This morning, I expected Darryn to try and convince me that she could drive herself to work from the station and not have the unmarked car following, but to my surprise she didn't. We drove to the station, she even kissed me goodbye. It was almost too easy, but I didn't have time at work to really think about it.

Charliee just left the station. We received a good lead today on the bombing case and wanted her to come identify the guy from a picture we were able to pull up. She did great but I can tell all of this is finally wearing her down. Since she has been seeing Travis, she hasn't needed Derrick and me as much. We are both happy she has found someone and Travis is a great guy, but I'm a little worried about her. We need to get this guy and end all of it, for all the families' sake.

"Hey, are you all right?" Derrick asks, sitting across from me at the table.

I hadn't even heard him come into the breakroom. "Yeah, just a lot going through my mind."

"Any word on the ex?"

I just shake my head.

"Are you sure that you're all right?" he asks again.

"I'm concerned about Charliee. She is trying to be so strong about all of this, but today I can see how tired she is. We need to find this guy. Charliee is strong but she is going to break soon." If I direct this conversation toward Charliee maybe Derrick won't ask me anymore about Darryn.

It's getting harder and harder every day to keep my marriage a secret. Right now is when I need to talk to him the most and I can't.

"Maybe we should talk to Travis..." Derrick is interrupted by another officer running into the break room.

"We have had another bombing," he informs the two of us.

"Where?" Derrick beats me to the question.

"Old abandoned building, which is what concerns all of us. It's not a normal target for him."

"We are going," I say as Derrick and I push past the officer standing at the door.

My phone goes off in my pocket. I ignore it. Then it goes off again. Pulling it out, I see Darryn's picture. I want to let it go, but something is telling me to answer it.

Swiping my screen, I answer as we are running out to the car. "Darryn, is everything all right?"

"Bryce, I'm sure you have heard about the bombing."

"We are on our way now, can I call you back?" We both slam through the door leading to the back lot where all the patrol cars are parked.

"Bryce, that's why I'm calling. We are here on the scene, we were called out."

Something is wrong, I can hear it in her voice. "Darryn, what's wrong? Are you all right?" I stop dead in my tracks.

"It's not me, it's Travis, Charliee's boyfriend," she informs me.

I want to be relieved she is all right, but the feeling is overtaken by now knowing something is still very wrong. Derrick is giving me a questioning look, I put my hand up telling him to hold on.

"Darryn, what do you mean it's Travis? What's going on over there?"

"We just got here, there was another bomb inside the building. When the firefighters went into the building it went off, trapping two firefighters inside. Travis is one of them."

"Damn it!"

"Bryce, what's going on?" Derrick asks from above our vehicle's roof.

"Darryn, keep me posted as you hear anything. We were going to come that way, but I think we are going to have to go to Charliee's, I don't want her hearing this some other way. Please be careful, there may be more."

I want to tell her to leave, but I know she can't. She has a job to do. Now I kind of understand what our parents go through with both Derrick and I being on the force.

"Poor Charliee, I will let you know anything I find out." She quickly hangs up the phone.

"Bryce, what the hell is going on? Is Darryn all right?"

"She's fine. There was another bomb in the building that went off, this time unfortunately there were firefighters inside. Derrick, Travis is one of the trapped."

"We need to get over to Charliee's," Derrick says then gets into the driver's seat.

He is backing out of the space when I reach the passenger side and get in. One of the hardest parts of our job is having to inform someone that something has happened to one of their family members. Those people you don't know though. Having to tell Charliee that Travis is trapped and we don't know if he is alive or not is going to be one of the hardest things we will ever have to do.

When we pull up to the house, we notice Charliee's Jeep isn't in the driveway. She and Jayden must have gone somewhere after they left the station today.

"She isn't home, we need to find out where she is." Derrick pulls out his phone to text her.

"Wait, here she comes, she just came around the corner. Who is going to be the one to tell her?" I ask, dreading this whole conversation.

Charliee pulls into her driveway, I can see the puzzled look on her face. Derrick opens his door and starts toward Charliee. I get out, but stay by the car. I can see Derrick's hands moving in front of him as he walks up to her.

I watch for a moment, Charliee asks why we are here. Derrick looks back at me with a look of dread in his eyes. I didn't say he was the one who had to do this, he just jumped out of the car. I see his head tilt back, Charliee is getting irritated, you can see it all over her face. Derrick doesn't need to do this alone so I walk up to join him.

"Charliee, maybe we should go inside," Derrick suggests.

"Where was it at, guys? What are you not telling me?" Charliee asks like she didn't even hear Derrick. He must have already mentioned the bombing.

"The explosion was at an abandoned building this time." Derrick is dragging this out.

Charliee's shoulders slump with relief, but then you can tell she figures out something isn't being said and she glares at both of us. "Dammit, guys, what are you trying to tell me? Just say it already, please."

Derrick places a hand on each of her shoulders and Charliee's relieved look moves to complete panic. Derrick looks her straight in the eyes. "Charliee, when the firefighters went in, a second bomb went off. Two guys from Travis's department are missing. Travis is one of them."

"Take me there," Charliee demands. She doesn't cry, she doesn't panic, she just starts walking toward our patrol car.

Derrick stops her by grabbing her shoulder and turning her around to face him. "We don't even know if it's safe, or if there is another bomb, Charliee."

This argument isn't going anywhere. Either we are going to take her or she is going to go alone. Derrick looks over at me for some help. "At least if she is with us, we can watch her," I suggest.

"Mom and Dad are going to kill us." Derrick motions for Charliee and Jayden to get into the back of the car. He stops her before she gets in though. "You need to promise us that you will stay with us."

As soon as we pull up to the building, Charliee starts barking orders to let her out. I get out of the car and open her door, but I block her from getting out. "You need to promise me you aren't going to do anything stupid, Charliee."

She just stares up at me. She is pissed but I don't care, her safety is more important to me than her being a little pissed off. "Promise me, Charliee, or I'm shutting the door and locking you in this car."

Honestly, I'm pretty sure she could shove me aside if she really wanted to right now, she looks pissed.

"Fine, I promise! Now move!" she yells at me.

I stand there for a moment and we just glare at each other. Finally, she starts to step out and I move out of her way. If Darryn was the one trapped in there, I would do anything to get to her. I have to put myself in Charliee's shoes right now.

I watch her for a moment as she just stands there, Levi standing in front of her, staring at the front of the building. My heart drops. I can't imagine what she is thinking right now. My sister has been through so much. She has always been a very strong person. She has never let being deaf stop her from anything, or ever used it as an excuse. Derrick and I have always been extremely protective of her, but as she grew up we realized she didn't need us as much as we thought she did. Since the night of the bombing that almost took her from us, I have noticed that she has tried to show she is good, that she is healing mentally and physically just fine. Physically I will give her, she was up and ready to go back to work long before the doctor released her, but mentally I have seen that the whole event has taken something from her. Travis has been her wall, the one she has turned to, not Derrick and me. It's been hard but I know Travis is a good guy and is taking care of her. If he doesn't make it through this, I'm worried for Charliee.

Jayden comes and stands beside me. "You know if anything happens to Travis, Charliee isn't going to bounce back from that very well."

I nod. "That's actually what I was just thinking myself."

"There hasn't been any chatter on the radio from inside of there?" she asks.

I just shake my head, everything has gone pretty quiet since they brought the other firefighter out. "The other firefighter is awake and talking to the paramedics, hopefully that's a good sign for Travis."

"Why haven't they pulled him out yet?" Jayden asks, but I know she isn't expecting me to answer. More just talking out loud.

I look over to see Darryn standing by her rig. "Hey, stay with Charliee, will you, Jayden? Make sure she doesn't go anywhere other than right there. I will be right back."

Jayden walks over to Charliee, I head over to Darryn.

"How is she doing?" Darryn asks as I approach her.

"Not good, I'm worried about her."

"Do you think it was the best idea to bring her here, Bryce? Who knows what to expect when they do find him." Darryn states the one thing I have thought since we agreed to bring her.

"Trust me, if we hadn't brought her then she would have come here on her own. This is the only option Derrick and I figured we had," I explain.

My phone vibrates in my pocket, pulling it out I see it's my mom. *Crap, here we go,* I think to myself. "Hi, Mom."

"What's going on, Bryce? We turned on the television and it's on every channel. Right now I can even see you and Darryn." My mom is panicking, but she hasn't said anything about Charliee yet.

Looking over my shoulder, I see all the news crews and cameras pointing in our direction. How the hell did they get this close? Sure, they have distance between them and the building but we have no idea if there are any other explosives and if so, where. I am about to tell my mom I have to go so I can talk to whoever is in charge of this whole mess when my mom yells on the phone.

"Bryce, why did that look like Charliee and Levi running into that building?"

What the hell? I turn around just in time to see my sister disappear into the opening, and hear Jayden scream after her. I don't even say anything to my mom, I shove my phone at Darryn and run to where Charliee disappeared.

Derrick reaches the entrance before I do, I follow behind him as we make our way over all the debris. It's hard to see but we can hear Levi's bark. Then we hear Charliee scream and we both stop dead in our tracks. We look at each other, listening. Levi has stopped barking, but somehow we hear Charliee's voice over all the other commotion as she tells someone she has found Travis and to hurry up. Both Derrick and I start in that direction.

Derrick reaches her first. She is sitting on the ground, Levi pawing at the debris in front of her, and she has Travis's hand in hers. I run a quick eye over her and that's when I notice her leg. It is bleeding badly and bent in a strange way.

"Derrick, look." I point for him to look at her leg. "We need to get her out of here."

Derrick grabs her shoulder to get her attention. "Charliee, let them do their job. I need to get you out of here, your leg is really bad."

"No, I'm not leaving him, Derrick, he hears me." Charliee pulls away from Derrick's grasp and turns her attention back to Travis.

Derrick looks back at me. As much as I want everyone out of this building, I can't say I blame Charliee for wanting to stay until they get him out. I nod to Derrick and we both get to work helping them uncover the rest of Travis's legs. The faster we get him out, the quicker we will get Charliee out.

What feels like an hour probably only took us no more than five minutes to finish getting Travis out. I look down at Charliee's leg, blood is starting to pool under it. Tapping Derrick on the arm, I get his attention.

"Her leg is bad, we need to get her out of here now."

Derrick nods. He turns to get her and that's when she tries to stand to follow the guys out carrying Travis, and her scream echoes through the building. Derrick quickly scoops her up in his arms and heads for the opening, I follow right behind.

Once we clear the building, they guys carrying Travis head to one ambulance while Derrick carries Charliee over toward Darryn.

"Derrick, no, you need to take me over to Travis, please," she begs him, but this time it isn't going to work. I can see her trying to look over Derrick's shoulder to see Travis.

Derrick's steps don't even hesitate, he just keeps right on toward Darryn who is waiting for us. I notice she has my phone up to her ear, probably still on the phone with my poor mom. I kind of threw it at her with her still on the line when I saw Charliee going into the building. She puts it down just as we reach her.

"I think the three of you just gave your mother a heart attack," Darryn informs us as we walk up and sit Charliee down on the gurney.

I give her an apologetic smile for leaving her to deal with my mom.

Darryn looks over Charliee's leg. "This isn't how I wanted to get to know you better, Charliee," she says, looking up at her, then gets busy cutting her pants.

I watch as Charliee's leg becomes more visible and notice it is a lot worse than I had thought inside. Now I want to kick myself for letting her stay. Who knows how much blood she has lost, and it is broken for sure.

I notice my phone laying on the bumper of the ambulance, my mom's picture popping up again. I reach to answer it but am stopped when I hear Charliee scream again. Turning around, I find her trying to get up from the gurney. Darryn is trying her best to control her but Charliee isn't having it, even though she looks like she is going to pass out at any moment. Something has her all riled up again.

Reaching across I try to help, but Charliee pushes against me. "Bryce, the bastard is here." She is now pointing over my shoulder.

Looking in the direction she is pointing, all I see are reporters. What is she thinking she is looking at?

I turn my attention back to her. "Who's here, Charliee, who are you seeing?"

Her face is pale, her eyes glassing over with tears, she looks terrified and pissed. "Bryce, he's here. He stayed and watched. Look at the guy standing next to the female reporter. He has on a dark blue sweatshirt. He's the one, Bryce."

Turning around once more, I find the guy she described right away. It is the same guy in the picture we had Charliee come down and identify earlier today. She's right, he stayed and watched. I don't want to spook the guy this time like we did at the fair. We can't let him get away this time. Turning so I don't seem to keep my attention on him, I bring my radio up and describe the guy.

"Jayden, you stay and help Darryn with Charliee, who knows what she will try to do," I say, then quickly turn and start walking in the direction of the guy. Derrick is by my side, I can see other officers moving to surround him. He isn't getting away today.

The closer we get to him, the more aware he is becoming. He is looking around, frantic like, and grasping a backpack he is wearing. What if he has another bomb? Before I can voice my fear to my brother, the guy takes off. He isn't getting away today. Both Derrick and I start after him.

Leaning my head over to my shoulder, I talk into my radio. "He is making a run. Derrick and I are right behind him. Block him in, but he is ours."

The chance isn't given to us. Before we know it, one of our K-9 units is outrunning us and I swear it happens in slow motion as we watch the dog jump up, grab the guy around the arm and drag him down to the ground. Derrick and I instantly stop, waiting for his partner to call him off.

Derrick and I watch as they roll him over and cuff the guy and just like that, it's over. We watch as someone from bomb control comes over and secures the guy's backpack. Standing him up, the officer starts walking in our direction.

"Sorry, guys, didn't mean to step on your toes, I had already released him when you came over the radio," the K-9 officer explains.

"Don't worry, probably better for it to happen this way," I state back, fighting the urge to pull my gun and just shoot the guy in the leg or something. Let him feel a little of the pain that he has put so many other people through. I know that really isn't a great thing to think, but I have to admit it went through my mind.

"They all deserved it," I hear the guy mumble under his breath.

Derrick and I lunge together. Who the hell cares if we wear the badge, now I just want to beat the shit out of the asshole! Before we can reach him, each of us has an officer holding us from behind and one in front, pushing us back.

"That guy better rot in jail for the rest of his life!" I hear Derrick yell next to me.

Jail is a little too nice for this guy, I think to myself.

CHAPTER TWENTY-FIVE

Darryn

Charliee is breaking my heart. She isn't talking or looking at me, but I can see the tears rolling down her cheeks. We hit a bump in the road and I watch her face scrunch up in pain.

I poke my head up into the front of the rig. "Hey, Tom, radio over and see if you can get any information on Travis, please."

"Sure, how is she doing? I'm trying to miss the bumps."

Patting his shoulder, I answer, "She is hanging in there."

Sitting back down, I look over at her dog, Levi. He hasn't moved. He just lays next to her, his head on her arm, and stares at her. I pat him on the head. "You are such a good boy."

He looks over at me from the side of his eyes and then

instantly back to Charliee. I tap Charliee on the arm, she slowly turns her head to me.

"He is a great dog."

She looks down at Levi, strokes his head a couple times and gives him a small, sad smile, but at least a smile none the less.

"Hey, Darryn," Tom calls up from the front.

"Yeah."

"They said he is still unconscious, but is breathing on his own. They just arrived at the hospital."

"Thank you, Tom."

We have to drive so much slower because of the severity of Charliee's injured leg. Looking back down at Charliee, she has her eyes squeezed shut. This job is so much harder when you know the patient.

Tapping her on the arm again, she opens her eyes. "They just reached the hospital with Travis, he is breathing on his own. That's good news."

"Is he awake?" Charliee speaks for the first time.

Sadly, I shake my head no. "Charliee, that doesn't mean it's bad."

"I should be with him."

"There is nothing you can do right now but wait, they wouldn't let you go back anyway. By the time we get you to the hospital and your leg taken care of, you will probably not have to wait long, if at all, to see him."

She stares at me for a moment, her eyes searching my face. "Do you love my brother?"

Now there is a question I wasn't expecting right now. I look at her puzzled for a moment. At first I don't think this is something we really need to talk about right now, but then after thinking about it for a moment, if it helps her keep her mind off Travis for a moment then I will talk about it.

I look to the front and notice Tom's head tilted toward us now. He heard Charliee's question. Looking back down at Charliee, I realize you never know when something in your life is going to change, it's too short not to live it fully.

"Yes, I'm very much in love with your brother," I admit out loud for the first time.

"I'm glad, Bryce deserves to be loved by a great woman. Don't get me wrong, I love both of my brothers more than words can say, but Bryce deserves it. He isn't out to play and send them on their way like Derrick can do. Bryce has never been like that. He wants the happily ever after, the family. Every time I have seen him look at you, I can see it in his eyes. You have caught him."

I don't know what to say. Charliee seems to think Bryce is in love with me from what it sounds like. My heart drops a little. If only she knew the whole story. I want to tell her how wrong she is, how he is only doing this as part of his job. I feel the ring against my chest and it's a constant reminder that we are only playing at this relationship.

I want someone to talk to and Charliee seems so easy to talk to. I am about to tell her she is so very wrong but Tom speaks first. "Darryn, pulling in now."

"Good news. We have finally made it. Let's get you inside, get that leg fixed up and you up to Travis, all right!"

Part of me is happy the conversation is over, but another part of me is a little disappointed that we didn't get to talk. I miss having girl friends to talk to.

Tom and I just finished getting Charliee transferred over into the care of the nurses and my phone is going off for the third or fourth time. Pulling it out, it's Karen. "Hello."

"Darryn, Jayden told me you were the one taking care of Charliee, how is she?"

I can hear the panic in her voice and can only imagine what Steven and she are going through right now. "We just got her in, it was a slow ride over because of the injuries to her leg. I can't say for sure but I know she will need stitches and my opinion is I think she broke it, but to what extent I'm sorry, I can't say."

"Okay!" She takes deep breath.

I can hear her repeat everything I just told her to Steven.

"Have you heard anything about Travis?" she asks next.

That's when it hits me, they have Kendall, that's probably why they aren't already here at the hospital. "Karen, I'm so sorry I didn't think about this earlier, you have Kendall! To answer your question, no, I haven't heard anything except he was breathing on his own, but still unconscious when they arrived here at the hospital, but you two should be here."

"I didn't want to bring Kendall down to the hospital," she explains and I feel terrible. They shouldn't be worried about taking care of my child when they should be here with theirs.

Looking at my watch, my shift isn't over for another two hours and Bryce is still working, but after he gets off he should be here, not worrying about Kendall or me. "Karen, let me call the daycare center real fast and make sure she is all right with you dropping her off there, you two should be here right now."

"I thought Bryce didn't want Kendall there right now?" I can hear the concern in her voice.

"Karen, she will be fine, right now it's more important that you are here. Charliee needs you."

Karen is quiet for a moment, I know she is torn right now

but it really shouldn't even have to be a decision. Charliee needs her here. "Let me call you right back." I hang up before she can say anything else.

Carrie over at the daycare is excited about seeing Kendall again. I text Karen and give her directions to the place.

Tom walks back in from restocking the rig. "Everything all right?"

"Yes, just trying to get everyone's information and get Kendall settled so that Charliee's parents can come down. I feel bad I didn't even think they wouldn't come here because they had Kendall. I'm sure Bryce is going to want to come here after he gets off. I'll meet him here after we get off, make sure everything with him is all right and then I will pick up Kendall from daycare. I already spoke to Carrie over there and she said she will keep her as long as I need her to.

"Are you sure that's all a good idea, Darryn?" Tom has concern written all over his face

"I really don't want Kendall hanging out here at the hospital if I can help it."

"I can go and pick her up and she can stay with us, I'm sure it would just break Heather's heart to have her around tonight," Tom says sarcastically.

Tom's wife is so sweet, but I don't want to put them out any more than I already am. "I appreciate the offer, but honestly I think Carrie may be mad if I don't let her stay. It's been a long while since she has been there, she was very excited when I called and asked about Bryce's parents dropping her off."

"All right, but if anything changes know the offer is still there." Tom starts out of the emergency room, me following close behind.

The last two hours of work seemed to drag by, and I haven't heard anything from Bryce except a quick text letting me know they did get the guy, and that he will have to stay at work a little later. I just text him back saying I will meet him at the hospital when he is done.

I have met Travis's parents briefly and his sister. Jayden, I have spoken to very briefly, but I think some other stuff is going on with her. She is here but her head seems to be somewhere else. She looks like she needs someone to talk to, but we really haven't met officially, except at the fair that night and that was just a quick introduction, so I don't ask any questions.

"Darryn." I hear my name from behind me. Turning around, I see Bryce and Derrick coming into the waiting room.

Bryce walks up and gives me a small kiss which surprises me, we have never shown any affection other than hugging when around people. I look around but no one seems to think anything of it, or maybe they were just not paying attention. His mom and dad are sitting with me, so he hugs them both as well.

I notice he is looking around, but for what I'm not sure. "Where is Kendall?" he asks.

"I had your mom drop her off with Carrie at the daycare. Your mom didn't want to bring her here to the hospital, and I agreed, but they needed to be here for Charliee and Travis. Carrie was more than happy to take her. She told me she was good with her until we head home, she figured we would want to be here until things calmed down a little and we learned a little more information."

He stares down at me. I can tell he isn't happy with the decision, but there weren't many choices to pick from really.

Maybe I should have let her go to Tom and Heather's, I don't think I would be getting the look I'm getting right now from Bryce.

"Bryce, she is fine. Would it make you feel better for me to go pick her up while you go up and see your sister and Travis?"

He stands there contemplating it. I can see him battling with which way he should go. Finally, he takes a deep breath and shakes his head no. "No, I'll go up real fast, make sure Charliee is doing all right and then we can go over together."

He looks exhausted, I have to hold back from going to him and wrapping my arms around him. "All right, I'll wait down here for you. While you are up there, I will call Carrie and make sure everything is all right and let her know we will be there to pick Kendall up in the next hour."

"Why don't you come up with me?" He is holding his hand out to me.

Shaking my head, I motion to the elevator. "I'm good, you go talk to your sister. When she is out and Travis is better, there will be plenty of time for me to get to know your sister better, right now I think she just needs her family."

Wrapping me up in his arms, he holds me tight and I feel his warm breath in my ear. "You are family."

I should be happy to hear him say that. I have never been part of a family really, but this one is only temporary. Tears burn the back of my eyes. I need to smile, Bryce doesn't need anything else to worry about right now except his family.

Pulling back, I turn him toward the elevator and give him a little push. "Go, I'll be good down here. Give Charliee a hug for me."

When the elevator doors close, I pull my phone out and call Carrie. It rings, and then rings again. That's strange, she usually answers pretty fast. After the fourth ring, I get her voicemail. I don't leave a message, she must be busy with something. I will give her a couple of minutes and try again.

Karen comes up to me, wrapping her arms around me in a hug. "You should have gone up with him."

Pulling back, I smile. "He needs time with his sister."

"You know he loves you, right?" Karen smiles at me, but there is a sadness in her eyes.

My heart slams in my chest seeing the disappointment in her eyes. "Karen, I'm sorry I have dragged your son into my problems. He deserves so much more than what I have got him involved with."

Karen is shaking her head the whole time I speak. "Darryn, I couldn't be happier that he picked you. You need to stop thinking he is doing all of this because it's part of his job. My boy is head over heels in love with you, it is written all over his face every time he looks at you."

That's exactly what Charliee said earlier today. If I am being completely honest with myself, I would admit that I know he has feelings for me. He has shown me every time we are together. I think he just deserves better than me and my problems that follow me everywhere. If I tell myself he doesn't care, then I can walk away from him.

"You know all of this, don't you?" Karen asks.

I can't even look her in the eyes. I can't admit to knowing it.

"And you love him!" It isn't a question, and when my eyes level with hers she smiles, the sadness in her eyes gone. "Darryn, you need to tell him, then you guys can stop living like this marriage is some dark secret and start enjoying a life together."

Start a life together? That won't be possible until Brett is out of my life and I know he isn't. He is around, why he is sitting so idle right now is what is puzzling me.

My phone vibrates in my hand, scaring me to the point I almost throw it across the room. Taking a deep breath to calm my racing heart, I look down and see Carrie's name on the screen.

"Hello."

Nothing. She doesn't say anything back.

"Carrie, are you there?"

Again, nothing back. I pull back my phone to see if the call dropped but no, it shows we are still connected. Putting it back up to my ear, I am about to try one more time with saying her name but I hear a faint noise in the phone. Hitting the buttons on the side, I make sure my volume is all the way up. Maybe she pocket dialed me. I am about to hang up and call her back but then I hear a voice over the line that causes my blood to turn ice cold and my heart to drop.

"Brett!"

No, this can't be happening. How did he know where Kendall would be? I try to listen to what is being said but it is hard, everything sounds muffled. How long has he been there? Are Kendall and Carrie all right? All these questions need answers and I need to get to my baby.

I reach into my pocket to get my keys and they aren't there. Where the hell did I put them? Thinking about it, realization hits me like a ton of bricks. I don't even remember grabbing them when I got out of the car. Are you kidding me? I don't have the keys to my car and Bryce is up with Charliee. I have no way to get to her. I want to scream.

"Darryn, what's wrong?" Karen asks behind me.

I spin around. "Karen, I need to use your car, please."

"Sure, honey. Steven, Darryn needs the car keys. Is every-thing all right?"

I want to yell hell no, everything isn't all right, but I just need to get to my daughter and now.

"Darryn, maybe you should wait for Bryce to come back down." Karen takes the keys from Steven and hands them to me.

I don't even answer her. I grab the keys, more forcefully than I probably should have, and run out to the parking lot. I want to scream when I realize I have no idea where they parked. *Calm down and think, the keys have a panic button on them.* Pressing and holding the button, I wait. The car's alarm sounds off in seconds.

I hear a voice from behind me. Turning, I see Bryce. Wait, no, that's not Bryce, that's Derrick.

"Darryn, wait!" He starts running in my direction.

This family has been through so much today, I can't allow him to get involved with all of this. Brett is my problem and once and for all I need to deal with him. I'm done running, I'm done looking over my shoulder. I'm done letting him run my life.

Getting in, I shut the door quickly, starting the car and pulling out. Derrick is next to the car as I start to drive forward.

"Darryn, stop and open the door."

"I'm sorry, Derrick, I have to go." I press down on the gas pedal and pray that I don't hit Derrick as I pull away.

Looking in the rear-view mirror, I see him running back into the hospital. He is going in to get Bryce. I know once Bryce finds out I left, he is going to be furious. I didn't tell anyone where I was going, he won't know where to find me. I feel bad because I know he is going to panic, but I need to fight this battle alone.

The drive to the daycare is only fifteen minutes from the hospital but I feel like it takes hours to get there. I pull up alongside the curb, parking behind a dark-colored car similar to the one that was following me that day. I jump out of the car, leaving the keys in the ignition. My phone is vibrating in my pocket again. It's been going off constantly for the past ten minutes or so. I know it's Bryce. Running up the walkway, I stop dead in my tracks as I reach the door.

Standing there, arms crossed over his chest, is the one man I had hoped to never see again in my life.

"Darryn."

"Where is my daughter?"

He unfolds himself and steps out of the doorway, stopping only a foot away from me. "You mean our daughter."

I want to scream in his face that she will never be his daughter, but right now I have to keep a level head. "Where is Kendall and Carrie, Brett?"

He motions with his head to the inside of the building. "Both inside and before you ask the next question yes, they are both fine."

My knees threaten to buckle with relief, at least they are both all right.

"We have all been waiting for you," he announces with a smug smile on his face.

That means he has been here awhile. This kind of surprises me, he had all the time he needed to take Kendall and run, why was he waiting for me to get here?

I'm all of a sudden very tired. I realize I'm over being afraid of him. "What do you want, Brett?"

He looks around and then motions for me to enter the building.

"If I go in then you need to let Carrie leave, she has nothing to do with any of this."

"Do you think you are in a position to be making demands?"

I take a step closer, closing the space between us. My skin crawls from being this close to him. Looking straight up at him, I repeat myself. "If you want me to go inside, then you need to let Carrie leave."

Brett laughs and it sends chills down my spine. "Wow, Darryn, you have grown a backbone. That's kind of sexy." He runs a finger down my cheek.

It takes everything in me not to flinch away from his touch.

His hand drops back down by his side. "Fine, the only reason I kept her was to keep the kid quiet. Actually, we will all be leaving now. You and the kid are coming with me. I'll be honest, I'm a little surprised you don't have that cop boyfriend of yours with you."

I can't hide the surprise that I'm sure shoots across my face when he calls Bryce my boyfriend. It causes Brett to laugh.

"Do you honestly think I don't know everything that has been going on? Come on, Darryn, give me a little more credit than that. I know you have been living with him, I even know where the house is. You drive to work with him every morning to the station and then you drive from there with an unmarked car following you and then that partner of yours follows you back to the station every night after your shift. An older couple has been watching the kid, I'm going to guess they are the cop's parents."

I want to throw up, he has been following me and he has

figured out everything. Why wait this long to make a move? If he calls Kendall "the kid" one more time, I'm going to slap him across the face. Before I can voice anything, he grabs me by the arm and pulls me inside.

Kendall spots me the moment I'm inside. She starts to run toward me, but Carrie holds her back and Kendall starts to cry.

"Keep her quiet," Brett snaps at Carrie.

"It's all right, Carrie, let her come to me." I pull my arm out of Brett's grip and bend down to catch Kendall, who is now running at me.

"Grab her stuff and let's get going," Brett says from behind me.

"Where are we going?" I ask, trying to waste time as I try and figure out a way out of this, plus with Carrie still here maybe he will give some information for her to hear.

"That's not important right now." Brett's voice is starting to become agitated. I need to keep him from getting mad, no telling what he will do then.

"Brett, you promised me Carrie could go," I remind him.

"Darryn, I'm not leaving you..."

"Carrie, you don't need to be a part of this," I interrupt her. If she is able to get out of here then that is one less person I have to worry about. I am pretty sure Brett isn't going to hurt her, but I don't want to take any chances.

"Darryn, do you honestly think I am going to just let her go before we can get out of here? I don't need her calling that boyfriend of yours before we can get out of town."

I screwed up, I didn't tell anyone where I was going because I wanted to handle this myself. Now I realize I made a very big mistake. I should have thought about Kendall. The main reason I ran to begin with and now I have basically handed her back to him. What did I think I was going to be able to do alone?

"Give the lady your phone and let's get going. I don't want you getting any ideas about trying to contact anyone, or anyone being able to trace your phone." Brett has thought of everything. This is why it took so long for him to make a move, he had been waiting and he knew I would mess up at some point.

"I'm so sorry, honey, Mommy messed up," I whisper to Kendall.

CHAPTER TWENTY-SIX

Bryce

It was hard to leave Charliee. I wanted to just sit there and hold her as she cried. She is tired and hurting again, this time just not physically. She is still one of the strongest people I know. If that had been Darryn laying there and me in Charliee's spot, I'm not sure I would be able to handle myself as well as she is. There is no question in my mind about how much Travis means to her.

When I step out of the elevator, Derrick basically runs into me trying to get on. "What's the hurry?"

"Man, I was on my way to get you. Darryn just left out of here in Mom and Dad's car and she was in a hurry."

What the hell is he talking about, why would she leave and with our parents' car? "Where was she going?"

Mom came up behind Derrick. "Honey, something is wrong. All I really heard was the name Carrie and Brett."

I feel like someone punched me in the stomach. Brett! Carrie is the daycare's owner, what is going on?

"Darryn and I were talking and her phone went off, when she answered she said the name Carrie. A moment later her face went white and I heard her say the name Brett. Bryce, who is Brett?" my mom asks, but I see it written all over her face, she has an idea who Brett is.

I don't need to answer her, she knows just by looking at me she has assumed right. "Bryce, you need to go find her."

"Would someone like to tell me what's going on, please?" Derrick cuts into the conversation.

I need to get to Darryn. "It's her ex!" I yell at him over my shoulder as I head for the doors.

Derrick is following me out and I'm happy to know I have the backup, plus he may have to make sure I don't do anything that's going to get me fired from my job, because so help me if that bastard has done anything to either one of my girls!

"I'm assuming when you say the ex, you are talking about the one she has been running from. What the hell is going on today? Is there a damn full moon or something and all the nuts are coming out?" Derrick runs to the passenger side of my car and gets in.

I don't say anything, I just need to get to my girls and fast. I am just hoping I'm not already too late. I throw my phone at Derrick. "Call her."

Come on, Darryn, pick up the phone, I chant over and over to myself as I watch Derrick put the phone up to his ear.

"No answer, it went to voicemail."

"Try again, and don't stop calling until she picks up," I command.

I never thought a fifteen-minute drive could feel so long, and even though we hit a number of red lights, I didn't stop for any of them. Damn, this would be so much easier if we were in the squad car. I would do anything for a siren right now.

Finally pulling up to the daycare, I see my parents' car parked along the curb. That is one small relief knowing this is where she went. Together, Derrick and I jump out of my car.

"What's the plan? Do we even know if they are still here?" Derrick asks as we approach the front of the building.

That's when the front door opens. I draw my gun, my brother following next to me. First, out comes Darryn holding Kendall, and then who I am guessing is Brett behind her.

"Hold it right there, Brett!" I yell, my eyes instantly locking with Darryn's. I see the relief flood over her face.

The world slows when I see him pull a gun from his back and point it straight into Darryn's side. Kendall starts crying and I have never felt more helpless than I do at this moment.

"Bryce, keep a straight mind," Derrick whispers next to me.

I'm trying, but seeing a gun being held on your wife makes things a little more difficult, I think to myself.

"She has no right to keep the kid from me, she is mine." Brett pushes the gun harder into Darryn's side and when I see her face scrunch up, I almost lose it.

Taking a deep breath, I try to remember our training and talking someone out of their gun, not acting fast and getting someone killed, good or bad guy.

"Well, as far as I'm concerned that's my wife and my child you are holding at gun point and I'm not going to allow you to take them from me!" I shout back.

From my side view I see Derrick's head whip around to look at me in shock. Darryn's eyes go wide and even from as far away as I am, I can see the tears form and fall down her check.

Suddenly, everything happens at once. Brett spins Darryn around to face him, then pulls Kendall from her arms as he brings the gun up and hits Darryn across the head with it. I watch as Darryn crumbles to the ground. Then the one word is cried out that I never understood until right now the impact it could have on a man.

"Daddy!" Kendall cries, her little arms out straight in front of her reaching out to me.

That one little word puts my feet into action. I'm not going to take a shot at the guy, he has my little girl in his arms, but I'll be damned if he thinks he is getting anywhere with her.

Shoving my gun into my back holster, I charge him, I don't care that the gun he is holding is now pointed straight at me. I will die before he hurts my girls anymore. I faintly hear my brother call my name as I see a figure come up behind Brett. It's Carrie. All at once I see her silhouette bring something up over her head and come around, hitting Brett in the back of the head. A shot from his gun goes off just before he falls to the ground, Kendall being dropped from his arms.

I hear Derrick yell my name, I see Darryn come to from the blow to her head, and I feel fire burning through my bicep. Reaching where Kendall fell and is now crying on the ground, I quickly pick her up, grab Darryn by the arm and basically drag her out of Brett's reach.

When I feel we are far enough away from any danger, I look over my shoulder and see that Derrick is putting cuffs onto Brett, while Carrie stands over him still with what I think is a bat over her head, ready to take another swing if need be. I can hear sirens coming down the street, it's over and my girls are safe.

Kendall's little arms are wrapped so tight around my neck I can barely breathe, but who needs to breathe, right?

"Bryce, you're bleeding." Darryn touches the side of my arm and pulls her hand away with my blood on it.

"I'm all right, it just grazed me." I look at my torn sleeve.

"How did you know where I was?" she asks.

"Mom heard you say Carrie's name and Brett's. It didn't take much to figure it out. But Darryn, this would have been a lot easier if you would have just told me what was going on. If something would have happened to either of you, I wouldn't have forgiven myself."

"Bryce, I'm sorry. I knew he was here and I couldn't let him take Kendall. Your family has been through so much, and with everything that happened today I didn't want to be the cause of anymore pain. Look, I got you shot." She points at my arm.

"Damn it, Darryn, when are you going to get it through that thick head of yours? You two are just as much a part of this family."

"Bryce, you married me to keep me safe..."

I can't believe after everything, that's what she still believes. "Darryn," I interrupt her. "I didn't have to marry you to keep you safe. Trust me, I would have figured out another way if that was all it was. I married you because from the day I met you I knew you were someone special. It didn't take long for me to realize I was falling in love with you."

"Seriously, man, first I find out you are married and then I have to watch you run full speed toward a man holding a gun at you. I'm not sure what I should punch you for first." Derrick comes up next to me looking a little pissed off.

Right now, I don't really want to deal with him. I just want to take the girls home.

"Hold that thought, Derrick." Darryn puts up a hand to stop my brother. "Did you say you are falling in love with me?"

"No, I'm not falling in love, I have completely fallen, Darryn. How have you not seen this already? I have done everything I could except say the words to show you how much you mean to me. But if that is all I haven't done then maybe this will make it sink in." I grab her by the back of the neck and bring my lips down to hers. Just before we kiss, I say against her lips, "I love you, Darryn, and I'm not letting you go." I then seal those words with a kiss that I hope expresses them to the fullest.

"I love you, too, Bryce." Darryn finally admits the one thing I have longed to hear from her.

"I love you, too, Daddy." Kendall's little voice breaks through our trance.

Darryn's eyes go wide at her little girl's words, then she looks away, almost embarrassed.

"Darryn, next to you telling me you love me, that is the next best word I could ever hear," I assure her.

"All right, now that everyone knows of the love, my turn. I have only one question. Does Charliee know about you two being married? Because I'll admit I'm a little pissed that I didn't know, but knowing what Charliee will have to say to you about it definitely makes it so much better." Derrick smirks at me.

I ignore my brother. "Come on, let's go home." I lead the three of us toward my car, I'm ready to take my family home!

"Come on, Darryn, we need to get going or we are going to be late for our own reception."

"Daddy, I'm ready." Kendall comes out of her room, twirling as she walks down the hallway in her what she calls "princess" dress. She has been so excited to wear it, we had to hide it in our closet so she couldn't get to it. If it was up to her she would be wearing it every day.

"All right, I'm almost ready, let me just go put on my shoes." Darryn comes out behind Kendall.

Derrick was right. When Charliee found out I had gotten married and hadn't told them, she didn't talk to me for a couple days, then she yelled at me! Basically she was mad because she had a sister and a niece she hadn't known about. Derrick was more disappointed I think than mad. Before this we told each other everything. I think this just proved to him that we do have lives that each of us might not know everything about. Trust me, I heard about it for about a week in the car at work and every once in a while when we see Darryn on a call, he will make some smart ass comment, but it's all right, all in all we are a family and I couldn't be happier.

Charliee and Mom insisted that since the whole family and our friends weren't at the wedding ceremony then we needed to have a reception, we didn't even argue it. I think Charliee being able to help Darryn with all the plans sort of made up for her not knowing.

"All right, I'm ready, let's go." Darryn comes flying out of our room and down the hall. My heart skips a little at the sight of her. I am one very lucky man.

When we pull up to the reception location, Charliee and Travis are waiting outside for us. Charliee is still sporting a walking boot, but her leg is healing quickly and she should be out of it in a couple weeks. Travis was lucky, he came out with a concussion and a few broken ribs. He was back at work two weeks after getting out of the hospital.

"It's about time you two got here, everyone is waiting inside. Let me go in and tell them you are here." Charliee turns and a fast as possible, walks back into the building, pulling Travis along with her.

"If it wasn't for your sister, I would never have gotten all of this put together," Darryn confesses.

Walking in, we are greeted with applause and congratulations from all of our family and friends. Kendall runs straight to Grandma Karen as soon as we walk in. Charliee grabs our hands and leads us over to the head table.

Dinner and toasts are started right away, honestly the evening is moving along in a blur. We are asked to take the floor for our first dance by the D.J.

Standing up, I hold my hand out to my beautiful wife. "May I have this dance?"

Taking my hand, Darryn smiles up at me and my knees almost buckle. Leading her out to the dance floor, I bring her into me, wrapping an arm tight around her waist.

"I'm sorry you never got a big wedding, I hope this makes up for that." I kiss her lightly on the lips.

"Bryce, this is all perfect. I wouldn't change a thing. Even the events of how we came together I'm thankful for. I know it sounds weird, but without my screwed up past, my life now would never be this amazing. I never imagined I could ever be as happy as I am with you."

This is the moment, I think to myself. Pulling back, I get down on one knee in front of her. You can hear all the gasps of surprise from the guests around us.

"Darryn, you have made this chase one of the best experiences of my life. I believe I started falling in love with you from the very first time you turned me down for a date and trust me, I asked many times and you turned me down each and every one, and each time my heart became yours a little more."

Pulling the ring box out of my pocket, I open it up and hold it up to her. "I'm not going to propose, I've already gotten the honor of making you my wife. I'm going to kneel before you and make you a promise. I promise to spend the rest of my life proving to you my love. Waking up every morning telling you I love you, and going to bed showing you my love every night. I promise to be your strength when you are in need of it, your best friend when you need someone to talk to. Darryn, there are no words that can express my love for you, but I plan to spend the rest of our lives proving it to you. I love you!"

Slipping the ring onto her finger, I stand up and wipe the tears away from her cheeks before I claim her lips in a kiss with promises filled within it.

"I have something for you as well." Taking my hand, she takes a step back from me and then places it onto her stomach.

All I can do is stare. "Are you serious?" I finally find my voice to ask.

She just nods.

"We are going to have a baby?" I ask in disbelief.

Again, she only nods.

Everyone around us is clapping and cheering but I only see my wife. This amazing woman who already gave me the gift of her love, a beautiful daughter, and now another child.

Crushing her against me, I claim her lips and she laughs against mine.

"I love you, Darryn!"

"I love you, Bryce!"

ABOUT THE AUTHOR

Tonya Clark lives in Southern California with her hot fire-fighter hubby and two daughters. She writes contemporary romance featuring second chance, sports, MC, shifters, suspense, and deaf culture—inspired by her youngest daughter.

When not hiding in the office writing, Tonya has the amazing job of photographing hot cover models, coaching multiple soccer teams, and running her day job.

Tonya believes everyone deserves their Happily Ever After!

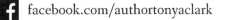 facebook.com/authortonyaclark

instagram.com/authortonyaclark

bookbub.com/authors/tonyaclark

amazon.com/author/tonyaclark

goodreads.com/tonyaclark

ALSO BY TONYA CLARK

Sign of Love Series

Silent Burn

Silent Distraction

Silent Protection

Silent Forgiveness

Sign of Love Circle

Shift

Fire Within (Coming Soon)

Raven Boys Series (Written by Multiple Authors)

Entangled Rivals (Book 3 Can be read as standalone)

Standalone

Retake

Driven Roads (Coming Summer 2020)

Anthology

Storybook Pub

Made in the USA
Middletown, DE
11 October 2020